INSIGHT PUBLICA

Kozhikode, Kerala, India 673011
www.insightpublica.com
e-mail: insightpublica@gmail.com
A Girl and the Tigers
(Children's Novel -English)
Cinasha
First Edition: December 2020

ISBN 978-93-90535-18-7
Cover Painting: Cinasha

A GIRL
AND THE TIGERS

Cinasha

CINASHA

Cinasha studying in eighth standard at Government Higher secondary School Kasaragod in Kerala. She was born on 29th October 2007 to Sreekumar and Smitha. Cinasha is interested in reading drawing and writing. Her two English novels 'The Mysterious Forest' and 'Song Of The River' were published on November 2019. She wrote the novel A Girl And The Tigers when she was studying in 7th standard.

Address: Cinasha, D/o Sreekumar A, Maipady (PO)
Kasaragod, Kerala, Pin : 671124
Ph: 9497842169, email: sreekumar2515@gmail.com

An Interesting Narrative

This novel is an interesting narrative representation by a twelve year old girl in writing and drawing... not a novel published after an appraisal by an editor's eye but published as a support for a young mind's interest and exploration. As her interest and exploration cannot be confined to the prison house of grammar, we have let her free of those syntactic shackles. We welcome you readers to this book so syntactically free and imaginatively rich. You won't be disappointed in reading it.

Sumesh Insight

CONTENTS

CHAPTER ONE

LITTLE GREEN ZOO

Genie could hear the music of the rain which was coming from outside. She loves to lay on her warm bed, eyes closed, listening to the sound of the rain. Genie Razi was a ten-year-old girl with shoulder-length brownish black hair and glittering black eyes.

Genie knew it would be eight o' clock in the morning. She knew that she have to get ready and go to school. It was a rainy morning. But she did not open her eyes. She continued to listen to the rain. She realized that the rain was getting heavier and heavier because its sound was getting stronger and stronger. It was already very late. Genie opened her eyes, and sat up in the bed. When she removed the blue blanket which was covering her and was giving her heat, she gave a sudden shudder. How cold it was! She quickly got out of the bed and ran to the bathroom.

After some time Genie got ready to go to school. She was in her school-uniform, bright blue shirt and black skirt. She picked up her purple umbrella which had silver flowers on it.

"Bye, Mum! Bye, Dad!" she said loudly in a cheery voice and jumped down from the verandah.

Genie started running, splashing muddy water, with her school bag shaking on her shoulders. She heard her mother and father hurrying to the varandah from inside the house and saying aloud: "Goodbye, Genie!" Genie looked back and smiled at her parents, her face being wet by the cold raindrops coming flying underneath the umbrella, as she was still running. She loves to run in the rain. She loves to run in the rain without any umbrella. But now, she don't want to stand outside the classroom, wet and staring at an angry teacher.

Genie's father David was a teacher. But not in her school. He was ill and not going for work today. Rachel, her mother had a coffee-shop in the town. She will leave the house soon in the black car. Genie's school was close to her house and she could walk to school from home and back.

Genie slowed down as the yellow building came into sight. She stepped onto the verandah, put her umbrella on the floor and entered the classroom which was very noisy with a lot of students playing and chatting to each other. Genie went to her seat and put her bag down and turned to look where Kevin Notts was. He was her best friend.

She found a tall boy with brown hair and a handsome face, chatting with two other boys.

" Hey, Kevin. " called Genie. Kevin and the other two- George Locs and Niaf Lee- stopped talking and looked at her.

" Hi" Kevin smiled and hurried towards her.

" Here you are! I was waiting for you. Then I met George and Niaf. I was really waiting - "

" Kevin, what's up? " asked Genie.

" Oh, nothing too serious. Today is Leda's birthday. " said

Kevin, happily. "Really? Why didn't you tell me, yesterday? Oh no! I don't have anything to give her, now. If you did tell me a word about it, yesterday, I would be able to prepare a gift for little Leda. But, now..." complained Genie.

"It doesn't matter, Genie. She had already got loads of gifts. Now, take this... " Kevin handed her a handful of chocolates.

" Oh, thank you. " Genie took them and said:

" Wish little Leda happy birthday for me. "

" Of course, I will " promised Kevin. Leda Notts was Kevin's younger sister. She was only three years old. Leda was in kindergarten. Genie liked cute naughty Leda very much.

Mrs Neila, their mathematics teacher entered the classroom. The classroom fell silent. It was sixth grade. Genie, Kevin and the other students hurried to their seats. Genie put the chocolates in her bag and pulled out her mathematics textbook and notebook.

Mrs.Riya Neila was very strict. Her thin arms and legs did not match to her fat, porky, round face. Mrs Neila's hair was long and brown. Most of the kids did not like her too much.

"Silence! Least common multiple is ...." Neila started teaching but Genie was not listening. She was listening to the rain...

Nothing happened on that day. Nothing but Antonella Foa, a girl with dark eyes-screamed loudly, at the sight of a hairy, ugly spider crawling on her seat, in the English period and made everyone jump.

✳ ✳ ✳

" You will have a trip to Littlegreen Zoo, tomorrow. Everyone who has their parents' permission would be able to come." Piya Sintra, their class teacher announced in the very next day, and the students started murmuring to each other, excited.

" So... " continued Mrs Sintra " We will leave at seven o' clock in the morning, tomorrow. We will be going in - "

" Oh please, it won't be Jola-Van... " muttered Antonella to Elsa.

" - we will be going in Darwin Jola's van! " as Mrs Sintra said so, the class broke into angry and disappointed murmurs.

" Oh, no... " said Antonella disappointed.

" I won't come... " murmured Sein violently.

" Why we always have to go in that ugly Jola-Van! " snapped Georgina angrily.

" It sounds great! " said Genie.

" WHAT? " jumped Kevin and George together.

" That - that ugly Jola-Van 'sounds great' to you? "

" NO! I hate Jola-Van. I was saying the trip to the zoo sounds great". explained Genie.

" Hmmm... "

Darwin Jola, their Grammer teacher had a van. A very old van. The students called that colour-faded, dirty, dusty van ' Jola-Van.' The Jola-Van always stinks as though it had never been washed.

"Ma'am, every time we had a trip to anywhere from our school, we had to use that horrib - er - I mean that van... " complained Genie.

" What do you mean, Miss Razi? " said Mrs Sintra coldly.

" Ma'am, why can't we just use our school-bus? " suggested Niaf.

" Don't be stupid, Niaf - " Genie began, but then Mrs Sintra said the exact same thing what Genie was going to say.

" Our school-bus will pick up the other students as usual, Lee. "

" But, ma'am - "

" OK, students. Let's go back to our lessons... " Mrs Sintra started to teach, ignoring Niaf's voice.

During the interval time, students of sixth grade were chatting happily about Littlegreen Zoo and angrily about Jola-Van.

"I heard that they had got a new tiger called Tio or Tino - or something like that - In the zoo. " said Sein Heartlo hopefully.

" A new tiger called Tigo. " corrected Nima Joa, knowingly.

"Oh, A NEW TIGER! " shouted Genie who felt losing the control of herself.

" What's too exciting with that, Genie? " asked Kevin surprised.

" WOOH! " Genie cried, her voice rising uncontrollably. Then she felt that she had got the control of herself back. She sat down on her seat, realising that she was jumping up excitedly, two seconds ago. What was happening to me? Genie felt sick.

She got to her feet and rushed out of the classroom. Genie knew Kevin will follow her and of course, he did. They stood under a tree. Genie stood next to Kevin, staring down at the earth.

" Are you OK, Genie? "

Genie looked up.

" You were shouting loudly and jumping when we talked about the tiger" explained Kevin.

" Ohh... " she felt more sick.

" I - I - I couldn't control myself... when the thought about a new tiger came into my mind, a very strange feeling came into my mind. You know, I love animals... especially tigers. Every time I think about tigers or see tigers, a strange, wild and uncontrollable feel of happiness comes into my mind... but this time, it grew wilder and wilder and - and... " Genie stopped, wondering how to express her feeling with words.

She looked at Kevin. He was staring into her eyes. Then these words fell out of his mouth: " I see... er - " The bell rang.

" GENIE! KEVIN! COME! " Antonella was calling from the varandah. Genie and Kevin walked towards her, silently.

Antonella waited until they reached the veranda. Then she stepped close to Genie, and Genie stepped back, nervously.

" What happened to you? " Antonella muttered in Genie's ear.

" What d'you mean? " Genie asked, but the truth was she knew what Antonella meant.

" When we were talking about the tiger, you jumped up and cried out, remember? What was going on with you, then? " Antonella whispered eagerly.

" I don't remember, " lied Genie.

" What? Tell me the truth, Genie... " Antonella murmured. Genie became angry.

" Antonella, that's none of your business! " Genie snapped. Antonella stepped aside and Genie and Kevin entered the classroom.

✶ ✶ ✶

Genie saw some of her classmates standing outside on the grass in front of the classroom as she walked towards them on the next morning. The yellow building and the excited crowd drew nearer and nearer...

" Hello, Genie, " said Elsa. Elsa was Antonella's best friend.

" Hi... " Genie smiled at Elsa's beautiful face. Antonella was there near Elsa. Antonella threw a nasty look at Elsa, and the smile on Elsa's face vanished, and she looked away from Genie.

Genie became nervous. She remembered that Antonella was not talking to her since she told her that was none of her business. Genie looked around to meet Kevin. But to her surprise, he was not there. Genie found George and asked him " Do you know where Kevin is? "

" No! " George said, not looking at Genie, because he was busy with chatting happily with a girl named Zoya Nee.

Genie stood there, and looked around. Everyone around her was talking and talking. She was the only one who was silent. Then, she saw Niva Joa and Nima Joa coming to her. Niva and Nima were the twin sisters from the Joa family. They looked exactly the same, but their attitudes were completely different.

" Hi, Genie, " said Niva. She was always happy, naughty and careless. But, Nima was always serious. Very serious. Genie smiled at them.

"Waiting for Kevin, aren't you? " Niva asked smilingly. Genie nodded at her. "He won't come, " said Niva. Genie looked at her. Niva grinned.

"What? " Genie asked in disbelief. " I - I mean - why? "

"Oh, he's ill... " said Niva carelessly.

"Flu, " said Nima seriously.

"He was OK till yesterday evening, " said Genie, surprised.

"Of course, he was. But, he fell sick at night, and the doc-
tor said he need rest" explained Nima.

" How d'you know? " Genie demanded.

" Niva told me, " said Nima. Genie looked at Niva.

" My Mum and Kevin's Mum are friends, you know, "
said Niva.

" So? " Genie raised her eyebrows.

" So, I heard his Mum talking to my Mum, " said Niva.

" From where? " Nima asked her.

" What? " Niva looked at her sister.

" Where did you hear them talking? " Nima asked clearly.

" Hee! I was hiding in the kitchen, " said Niva, grinning
widely. Nima turned her face away with dislike. Genie became disappointed, knowing her best friend will not be
with her in the trip.

"OK, students... " hearing this, Genie looked up, and saw
Mrs Sintra coming, her hands rubbing together. She was
wearing a yellow gown with white dots. She threw one of
her hands into her pocket, and pulled out a piece of paper.

" Wez, William " she called, looking at the list. William, a
boy with smiling face stepped forward, and stood near Sintra.

" Leven Ivan... Joa Nima... Joa Niva ... " she was going
through the list of students who told her they would be in
the trip.

Then, she called : " Notts Kevin " and Genie said nervously :

" He is ill, Ma'am. "

Sintra took a red ink pen, and marked something on
Kevin's name in the list. The list went on and on. Genie was
not paying attention.

" Razi Genie, " she heard Sintra's voice as though it was a voice coming from some other world. " Razi Genie! " This time, the voice was clearer and louder, and then, looked up to see an angry Sintra staring at her. Genie stopped thinking about Kevin and stepped forward.

" Everybody's here except Kevin Notts and Maria Yumia, " said Sintra, looking at the students from the list.

Then, a van came screeching towards them. Everyone looked at it. Ugly Jola-Van stopped with a loud screech in front of them. Mr.Jola was in the driving seat.

" Uh-oh! Ready for a bumpy ride, " whispered Niva in Genie's ear.

" Hmmm... " Genie murmured back.

" Be silent, Niva, " commanded Nima.

All the students tried to rush into the van at the same time, and it got totally worse. Sintra and Jola tried to control the children, but they could not.

At last, all of them got into the van. Genie was disappointed because she did not get the window seat. She was not sitting near the window. She was sitting between Niva and Nima. Genie always loved to sit near the window in any vehicle, with the feel of cool wind whipping her hair.

But then, Genie broke into an excited conversation with Niva about Tigo the new tiger.

"Isn't it exciting" the one who spoke first was Niva.

"What?" asked Genie in a bored voice. She was still thinking about the seat near thw window that she missed.

"The new tiger", replied Niva with a wise glance at Genie.

"Oh, that! Exciting? It is enchanting!" said Genie loudly in great wonder. Her mood changed so suddenly from dull to amazement. And it was clear, that was what Niva was hoping for.

"Yeah, I hope the new tiger- I believe it's name's Tigo.- is wonderful" said Niva hopefully. At this point, Genie gave a short laugh. Then the strange feeling like having a roaring ocean inside came to her making her stop laughing.

"Every tigers are wonderful, Niva!" said Genie, managing to keep a smile.

"Maybe you're right," said Niva shaking her shoulder.

Giene smiled and looked away to stop the conversation. She was doing so because the ocean in her was roaring so wildly and she was afrid about about it flooding out as she continue to talk about the tiger. Fortunately, Niva didnot talk more.And the strange happiness and the feeling - the feeling like having a roaring ocean inside- came into Genie.

Finally, Jola-Van stopped in front of the huge gate of Littlegreen Zoo, and the children jumped out, relieved because they were feeling so uncomforted in the dirty van through a bumpy ride.

The children began their walk through the zoo as a line. Sintra and Jola were leading them. They were suffering with their hard-work to keep the children silent and make them walk in a straight and correct line. And of course, they failed, because no child can stay silent while seeing a beautiful bird or an exciting animal.

First, they watched birds. Beauteous peacocks made them yell with their birdy dance. Doves made the little ones more light hearted. Parakeets and Macaws made them laugh. Those birds were chirping just like the children were. Eagles were royal looking and Owls were mysterious and were still being the symbol of wizardry and witchcraft with their strange eyes glittering coldly. Some of the kids including Genie were those who belive that Owls are the creatures with the strangest eyes in the whole world.

Then they saw a signboard saying that they had came through the section of birds and now they were going to to see the animals. Suddenly, a wave of murmurs appeared in the crowd of the students, as someone said they were going to see the new tiger Tigo.

Genie's heart started thumping very loudly. Sweat appeared on her face. She did not know why she was being very tensed. The strange feeling came to her mind again. She was afraid if she would lose the control of herself, again.

The large ironic cage drew nearer and nearer... now, they were going to see the tiger in it, and Genie's heart sank. She saw a large tiger walking round and round in the cage. It was Tigo. Genie felt the strange feeling growing wilder and wilder...

How attractive that animal was! Its face was a royal one. It had white whiskers that made it cute. Its brownish orange fur was striped in a beautiful pattern. Its tale was waving in the air. Its legs were strong and paws were big and strong but also soft. The big tiger was attracting Genie towards it like a magnet. Genie felt the ocean in her mind roaring more loudly... and then - she found herself face to face with the tiger. Her face was clutched to the ironic bars of the cage, and the tiger called Tigo was staring at her. She stared back. She gazed into the small eyes of Tigo. He was not blinking. Genie did not blink, too. Tigo's eyes were coloured in a wild green and brown. They glittered. Genie could feel the warmth of the breath of the tiger.

Then she heard people behind her screaming and shouting. But, she felt those sounds so misty as though they were coming from far away... far, far away... far, far, far, far away...

Someone's arms came to her and tried to pull her back. But, her hands were clutched to the bars, very tightly, and she did not want to get away from Tigo.

Then, came more arms to her. And those arms pulled her back, more powerfully. And at last, Genie's hands got away from the bars. As Genie got away, the tiger blinked, and laid down on the floor of his cage.

Genie felt the ocean in her mind suddenly stopped roaring, so, she could hear what the shocked crowd was saying. She knew the arms that pulled her back were the arms of Sintra and Jola, because she was now facing them, nervously. They were very red and angry.

" WHAT HAVE YOU DONE? ARE YOU MAD? " they started shouting at her. And then, the guards of the zoo came hurrying to them. Sintra dragged Genie roughly through the crowd towards the Jola-Van, while Jola started explaining the guards what had happened.

Genie was sitting on her seat, her head bowed down, her classmates around her asking her a lot of questions about why she had done a strange thing in the zoo yesterday. But, Genie did not answer any of it.

She wished to meet Kevin. She need to share her experience with him. She had not told her parents what had happened in the zoo.

Then Kevin came hurrying to them, fighting his way through the crowd.

" What's going on here? " he shouted and the crowd fell silent.

" Genie, " he called, throwing his bag onto his seat. Genie stood up and walked to the veranda with him.

" I've got something to tell you, " both of them said at the same time.

CHAPTER TWO

ANTONELLA,
MERINA AND THE PAPER SLIP

Kevin and Genie stared at each other. After a while Kevin asked.

"What is it, Genie?" Genie did not say anything.

"Genie, tell me what you've got to tell me" said Kevin.

"Oh, yeah" Genie told Kevin all about what happened in the zoo. Kevin was surprised and excited to hear it. And then she asked

"What you've got to tell?"

"Oh, that -" Kevin looked around to make sure that he was not being overheard.

"Genie, you know, I was staying home because of my flu," said Kevin.

Genie nodded.

"And today I felt OK and decided to come to school. When I was walking to school, I saw a" - Kevin had to stop there because Mr. Neila, their teacher came to the classroom and he and Genie ran back into the classroom.

Genie and Kevin sat down on their seats. Neila began to

teach and then Genie hissed in Kevin's ear "Kevin, tell me what you'd seen on the path, today morning"

Kevin muttered "It was ...."

"What're you doing, Mr. Notts?" Neila said sharply to Kevin.

"N-noth-nothing maam" Kevin lied.

"And you Miss Razi..." Neila looked at her.

"Nothing, Ma'am!" Genie repeated.

"Hmm... listen to me when I'm teaching..." Neila continued the lessons.

"Kevin, tell me..." Genie whispered.

"It was - it was a girl!" said Kevin.

"Oooh! What's extraordinary with that? I thought you had seen something strange." said Genie in a half-disappointed and half complaining voice.

"Of course, it was strange." Kevin hissed. Genie looked at him.

"She was sobbing!" said Kevin.

"Sobbing?"

"Yes and she was a stranger. I had never seen that girl anywhere, before. She was sobbing, her face in her hands. And..."

"What had she did when she saw you?" Genie asked eagerly.

"She looked up and asked that if I know a girl named Genie Razi" Hearing this, Genie froze. She became speechless. She stares at Kevin's face. "W-W-What?"

She said at last. "No ! It couldn't be. You're kidding!" said Genie.

"No, I am not", said Kevin.

"Are you sure? Why did she want to see me? How did she know my name? Who was she? What did she look like? Pretty? Or -"

"Wait, wait, wait..." Kevin stopped her shooting loads of questions to him.

"When that strange girl asked me if I know Genie Razi, I asked her who she was. Then she shouted to me angrily I don't have any right to ask her any questions. And then that girl stormed away, sobbing again... she had long red hair. Yes, pure red... deep red...." said Kevin, his eyes were fixed on the little bit of dark, rainy sky, that was visible through the short wooden window.

Genie said nothing. She did not pay any attention to the rest of the lessons. She was sitting on her seat, motionless, staring at the little bit of stormy sky through the small window. Her arms were resting on the desk.

When it was evening, their school time was over, Genie took her school bag and walked out of the classroom. She heard Kevin hurrying to catch up with her. Genie said nothing to him. They walked in silence. Then they got the place where the way split into two and Genie have to take left and Kevin have to take right to reach their houses. "Bye!" said Kevin and he began walking through the path on the right side.

"I m coming with you!" Genie said seriously and started to walk with him. Kevin looked at her, puzzled.

"I wanna find out about that mysterious girls!" Genie explained.

"Er-why don't we try tomorrow?" said Kevin.

"Are you scared? If you're not keen to come, fine. Just go straight to your home. I can find out on my own!" said Genie very sharply and Kevin said

"Of course, I will come; fine..."

They reached a narrow path. "She was standing there." Kevin pointed at a narrow gap between green bushes and the stony path.

"Let's search for her!" Genie and Kevin broke into search for the strange girl.

They searched and searched. They searched beyond the bushes, along the path, under the walls, between the trees... but there was no one except two persons. And those two persons were Genie and Kevin themselves.

"Let's stop this, there's no one here" said Kevin in a tired voice. "Let's go home" he said.

"Right" said Genie.

But her voice was proving that Genie did not want to go back. Then Genie's eyes caught something.

"Wait, Kevin.." she walked towards the bushes.

Kevin stood where she left him and watched her. Then she bent down over a green bush which was very large and dark. She tried to see what's inside there. As she moved the leaves aside with her arms, the sunlight flowed into the bush. The inner leaves of the bush were shivering a little, as though they were touching or seeing the drops of sunlight for the first time in their lives.

By the help from the sunlight made Genie saw it through the green leaves.

"It was a Trapdoor, A TRAPDOOR!" Genie yelled at sight of a trapdoor under the bush.

"Kevin come and see!" she yelled and he ran to the bush.

"Where?"

"Here"

"Ohhhh" his eyes widened in amazement.

"What's going on, here?" asked Genie to herself in dis-belief.

"Open it... open it.." she heard Kevin muttering in her ear.

"Come on, let's open it!" said Genie and she sat down. So did Kevin. Their fingers moved towards the trapdoor slowly... very slowly... she saw his fingers shivering.

The trapdoor was going to be opened.... but then-

"STOP! DON'T OPEN IT! STOP!" they heard a loud cry from behind them and both of them looked back. A girl was running towards them, yelling. She looked very worried. Genie and Kevin sat there, frozen to see who it was.

"Maria! Maria..?" Genie muttered under her breath. Yes, Maria Yumia, their classmate was running to them. Maria's deep blue eyes looked very tired. She reached there and pulled Genie. She dragged Genie and Kevin away from the trapdoor.

"HEY!" Genie removed Maria's arms from her and stood up. Kevin got to his feet, too.

Silence....

She and Kevin stood, staring at Maria Yumia. Maria stood, staring back blankly.

"Maria, why're you here?" it was Kevin who broke the silence.

"Why're you here?" asked Maria back, sharply.

"Maria, w-" Genie began but Maria gave a 'shhhhh' and Genie fell silent.

'To where that trapdoors leading? Why was that mysterious girl Kevin had seen in the morning sobbing? How did she know Genie? Why maria was here? Did Maria know something about that girl? Or about the trapdoor?' a flood of questions came roaring into Genie's mind. She looked at Maria to ask. But Maria said

"Go!"

Genie opened her mouth "But.."

"Can't you hear me? CAN'T YOU HEAR ME?" yelled Maria angrily. Her black hair and green frock started shaking violently at her yells.

"Of-of course!" Kevin said in a whisper.

"THEN I SAY GO! I SAY GO! LEAVE, NOW! RIGHT NOW!" Maria's yells echoed on the walls aside the path. There was no one on the path except a scared Kevin, puzzled Genie and an angry Maria. Kevin pulled Genie's arm and dragged her away, quickly.

"She's mad!" he murmured as they walked away.

"Stop!" came Maria's shaking voice. They looked back.

"Don't tell anyone about what you had seen here, Got it?" said Maria. Genie saw Kevin nod.

"Now go, without looking back" she commanded. Genie and Kevin walked until Maria was out of sight.

"What's wrong with her?" Kevin had no answer for Genie's question.

"She didn't come for the Littlegreen trip, yesterday. She and you were the only two who didn't attend the trip" Genie told Kevin.

"Hmmmmm" he nodded thoughtfully.

"We can ask Merina!" Merina always seemed mysterious and everybody believes she was keeping so many secrets.

"Yeah, we'll ask her..." Genie said, determined.

"Now it's too late and we must go" Kevin was worried.

"Oh, yeah... Bye.." Genie said carelessly and gave a run to her home.

Genie did not stop running until she got to the varandah of her house. She threw her shoes away and put her bag down on the floor. She opened it and pulled a key out of it. Genie opened the door and she stormed in, dragging her bag. She placed the key on the table and went straight into her room.

Without changing her uniform or washing her legs, Genie jumped into her bed. She pulled out a white paper and a pen.

Trapdoor, she wrote

Maria Yumia

next-

Merina Yumia

She finished writing and went to wash her legs. Genie knew her parents would not return until 6 o' clock in the evening, everyday. Her father had became well and healthy again and he had gone to work today.

After washing her legs and changing her dresses, Genie threw herself into her bed. She laid there first staring at the blue pictures of flowers on her blanket. And then she laid, staring at the white ceiling.

'First the trapdoor...' she thought - 'and then Maria Yumia... and next coming Merina....'

Genie got out of bed quickly when she heard the sound of a car coming to the front of the house. She put the paper in her bag and walked out to meet her parents.

* * *

"Kevin!" Genie stepped into the classroom on the next day, calling Kevin. Kevin was dropping his bag on his seat. She guessed that he might be just reached the classroom then. He looked at her. She walked towards him and put her bag down.

They looked around to see where Marina is.

"There!" said Genie pointing at a girl with deep blue eyes, sitting near the window, in a serious conversation with Antonella. Genie and Kevin got nearer.

"...but I don't like them.." said Antonella.

"Don't be stupid. There's nothing to be scared of them. And "Shhhh..." Antonella stopped. Merina and both of them looked at Genie and Kevin, questioningly.

"Er-Merina-er-Merina, we want to talk to you!" said Genie nervously.

"Of course, you can!" said Merina with a misty smile.

"Er...." Genie looked at Antonella. Antonella quickly got to her feet and stormed away.

"What's it my dear Razi and Notts?" A misty smile was still in there in Merina's face.

"We're going to tell you a secret. You won't tell this anyone, would you?"

"Of course, I would not! you know, I have a special skill to keep secrets.... ha!" said Merina, her smile widening.

"We saw a trapdoor and when we tried to open it, your sister came and stopped us!" said Genie very fastly. Merina looked shocked and the smile had disappeared from her face.

"You're jocking...." she said.

"No, we aren't jocking! It's true!" said Kevin.

"Merina, why your sister didn't come for the LittleGreen trip?" asked Genie in a whisper.

"She was ill!" said Merina.

"Or at least she told me she was ill!" she added.

"Ok, ask her about that trapdoor. If you get any information, tell us, Ok?" said Genie. Merina nodded.

"Merina, have this!" said Antonella walking towards them with some papers filled with alphabets written by someone. Genie gave a quick look at it and she caught one word from those: Tiger.

Merina immediatly took those papers and pushed them into her pockets. "Thanks, Antonella..." Merina said and Antonella grinned and walked away. Antonella was still not talking to Genie.

"Merina, what's written in those papers?" Kevin whispered, watching Antonella getting away, as though he was making sure that she was not able to hear him.

Merina smiled a most misty smile and walked away to catch up with Antonella.

Genie and Kevin looked at each other.

"Hey, look!" Kevin said pointing at the floor.

"What?" Genie saw a little slip of paper, laying on the floor.

"It felt out of Merina's pocket!" Kevin whispered.

Genie and Kevin ran and took it from the floor. The slip of paper had only two sentences on it, in a neat handwriting.

'I killed her... yes, I killed my Anne... '

She and Kevin stood there, horrorstruck. Their hands began to tremble. Their fingers shivered and the paper slip fell down from their hands. Both of them stood there, staring at the small slip of paper that was laying on the floor. Then they stared at each other, horrified...

Genie saw Kevin's face being covered in sweat. His face was very white as though the blood in his face had flooded away. His eyes were fixed on her own eyes. She felt sweat appearing on her face, too.

After a while, Genie bent down over the floor and picked the paper slip up. Alfred Minaz, their history teacher, stormed into the classroom, already angry and became more angry to see the classroom untidy. He started shouting and snapping.

Everyone except Genie and Kevin hurried to their seats. She and Kevin were still standing there shocked.

"Are you deaf, Mr. Notts? And you, Miss Razi? Can't you hear me?" he turned to them.

"Oh, yes sir!" said Genie quickly and she tried to push the bit of paper into her pocket, but Mr. Minaz's sharp eyes caught it.

"Aha! A letter! is that a love letter, Miss Razi?" said Minaz in a dirty voice and some of the students laughed. Genie went red. Very red.

"Give it to me! Let me check!" he said. Genie looked at Antonella. She said something and Genie guessed it would be 'no' by the way her lips moved.

"Razi, GIVE IT TO ME!" Minaz's voice was rising un-controllably..

"No sir! This is not a letter! It's just...."

"Then throw it out!" Minaz said coolly to Genie. She clutched the paper between her fingers, tightly.

"You said it's not an important thing! So, rip it into bits and throw it out!" commanded Minaz. Genie thought about it. If she don't do what she had been told, Minaz will read the words that was written on the mysterious paper piece and it will get her and Kevin into a lot of troubles.

She looked on Kevin, puzzled.

"Do what he had said!" he hissed. She ripped the paper into so many little bits. She walked towards the window. She stretched her hands out and then there was a pause, and now the little bits of paper were lying on the mud, being wet in the rain, outside the classroom.

Genie took a deep breath and turned to face Minaz.

"Good, Razi!" he said with a nasty smile.

Genie and Kevin sat down on their seats. Genie felt Antonella and Merina staring at her from their seats but Genie did not look up to face them.

"Minaz was right! It's a letter!" said Kevin and Genie stared at him. They were walking home after school.

"I mean, that slip of paper would be letter!" Kevin repeated.

"What did you mean?" asked her in a puzzled voice.

"A short letter by Antonella to Merina!" explained Kevin in a sort of I-understood-it-all voice.

"So, you mean that Antonella had killed a girl named Anne?"

"Perhaps Anne was a cat or a parrot or something like that. I don't think that Antonella would dare to kill a girl."

"Hmmm.... that's right. She wrote that 'I killed my Anne', remember - her Anne. That means Anne was someone she loved a lot..."

"But why did she killed her, then?"

"No idea, Kevin!"

"Ok, bye then." Said Kevin as they reached at the place where the way split into two.

"Let's go and open the trapdoor." suggested Genie.

"Er-we can go tomor-er-fine." said Kevin, seeing Genie throwing to him a sort of we-will-go-and there's no other choice look.

Genie and Kevin were walking through the path, where the green bush stood hiding a very secret trapdoor inside it. They reached the dark bush and parted its leaves aside with their arms and looked eagerly at the trapdoor on the grassy ground.

Their arms moved towards it. It's going to be opened soon by a little girl and a little boy. Their hearts were thumping very loudly. The trap-door was going to be opened... Then-Genie's heart sank-the trapdoor opened. Not by her or Kevin, but by someone inside it. They gasped as a head poked out from under the trapdoor.

A girl's head with long red hair. Deep red... pure red...

"You..?" gasped Kevin.

"Yes, me!" smiled the girl who opened the trapdoor one minute ago. She climbed up from under the trapdoor and stood before Genie and a shocked Kevin.

"Hello, Genie Razi." said the strange girl to Genie's surprise.

"H-h-how-how do you know my name?" she heard herself asking.

"Ha! what a question! I know many things about you! Not only your name. You're Genie Rasita Razi. Your father is David Razi, a teacher and your mother is Rachel Razi who runs a cafe in the town. You are ten years old and studying in sixth grade, Nelashtran School. Your best friend is Kevin John Notts. And-and-and you have a strange feeling when you see tigers..." said the girl, the last sentence with a misty glance at Genie.

Genie stood there, frozen, her mouth hanging open. She turned her head towards Kevin and gazed at him.

"This-this girl is the one, I told you I had met one morning" he said, without looking at her, still gazing at the strange girl.

"Who are you?" it was Genie who broke the silence. The girl laughed aloud.

"Who are you?" Genie repeated. But the girl continued laughing even more loudly.

"WHO ARE YOU?" Genie's voice raised very highly, annoyed. The girl suddenly stopped laughing. Her eyes started to burn. Genie gasped. Kevin gave a shudder. The strange girl gazed at them with burning eyes. Her eyes were turning red.

"WHO AM I" she thundered and Genie took a step back.

"WHO AM I? A GIRL! A TIGER-GIRL ......" she suddenly stopped shouting and burst into tears. She turned to the other side and started sobbing. Now Genie and Kevin could only see her back. She gave loud sobs.

Then it started raining. Large and heavy rain drops started falling. The girl's sobs grew louder. Genie and Kevin looked at each other. Then they walked slowly towards the sobbing girl.

"Are you ok?" asked Genie with half pity and half fear. The girl didn't answer and continued weeping. Genie slowly moved her arm towards the girl's shoulders which shook up and down as she sobbed.

"A - are you O - " the girl suddenly turned to face them and they jumped back.

"Oh, sorry I didn't mean to scare you." she said smiling and she looked completely normal now.

"Hi, I'm Rose Rose Ginch." she said brightly and Genie noticed that she had seen that beautiful smile somewhere before.

"What's a Tiger-Girl?" Genie couldn't stop herself asking.

"Oh, a Tiger-Girl! Ha! it means-" Rose Ginch stopped there as though enjoying Genie's and Kevin's curiosity.

"Tiger-girl!" Rose whispered.

"Tiger-girl?" said Genie and Kevin at the same time.

"Yep. There's so many Tiger-Girls in this world. I am one of them. Each Tiger- people have a tiger. A Tiger-Girl's or Tiger-Boy's soul's connected to the soul of her or his tiger. Every Tiger-One have to find their tiger."

"T-Tiger- people have magic powers?"

"Of course, we have. But it's called Tiger-Powers. The powers tigers have and some extra powers. Every tiger in the world have a Tiger-Girl or a Tiger-Boy...."

"I am a Tiger-Girl, I told you. And my tiger is Toma..." a strange glittery flash came to Rose's eyes as she uttered the name of her tiger. She continued-

"And-and my Toma's in LittleGreen zoo.." Rose sighed.

"LittleGreen zoo?"

"Yes. And I'm - I'm going to rescue her!" said Rose in a misty tone, her eyes narrowed. Genie gasped. She saw Rose's eyes glittering strangely.

"Oh, bye!" Rose said swiftly and without a warning, she jumped down through the trapdoor and closed it.

Genie and Kevin quickly ran forward and tried to open the trapdoor. But alas! Rose had locked it from inside. They pushed it. But it did not work. They started to pound violently on the wooden trap door.

"Rose... Rose...! Rose, OPEN THE DOOR! ROSE...." shouted Genie very loudly that Kevin took one of his arms back from the trapdoor to cover one of his ears.

"ROSE! ROSE!" yelled Genie, pounding on the trapdoor louder than ever that now Kevin is sitting both of his hands covering his ears very tightly and his eyes closed more tightly.

"ROSE! ROSE!" Genie gave a hard pound and stopped pounding and yelling. She sat on the grass, disappointed, panting, her fingers aching.

"Oh..." she gazed at her own fingers which had been very pink by pounding so hard continuously on the rough trapdoor. Kevin took his arms off from his ears, looked at her fingers and then at her face.

Her face was wet by sweat. The edge of her nose and her cheeks seemed glowing pink in the sweat drops. She got her breath back and then they heard someone moving under the trapdoor. Kevin looked at Genie, afraid about what Genie was going to do.

She did the exact same thing Kevin had feared of. She started pounding and shouting again.

"ROSE! ARE YOU THERE? RO-"

"I am here, Razi!" said a cold frozen voice from behind them. She and Kevin looked back and found themselves staring at Minaz.

Genie froze and she knew Kevin was froze, too.

Then there was a pause. After a while they stood up

quickly.

"What are you doing here?" Minaz asked.

"Nothing" Genie lied. Minaz threw a look at the trapdoor behind them and Genie's heart sank.

"Hmm..." said Minaz.

"What's that?" he asked. They said nothing.

"I'll see..." Minaz walked slowly towards the trapdoor.

"No, sir. It's nothing sir" said Genie and Kevin and they tried to stop him. He smiled and continued to walk.

"Sir, sir, Please sir!" their voice were shaking.

Minaz got near the trapdoor and they stood there breathing heavily.

"Aha! Nice!" Minaz bent down over the trapdoor. Genie's heart sank. To her and Kevin's surprise, Minaz called softly-

"Rose.... Rose... Come on.." Genie and Kevin looked at each other.

Then suddenly, the trapdoor opened and Rose climbed out. Her face was very pink by crying all these time.

"Oh dear, don't cry..." said Minaz, kindly. Tears splashed down through Rose's cheeks. She gave loud sobs and laid down on the grass and started squealing.

"Still thinking about Anne?" said Minaz.

"Anne... sh..she killed my Anne... oh..no... I-I-" Rose couldn't continue any more that she broke into loud sobs.

"Razi, Notts go" commanded Minaz and without a word, Genie and Kevin left.

Genie and Kevin got to Kevin's home, after a silent walk. She sat down on an armchair and drank a glass of water that Kevin had gave her. She knew his parents wouldn't return to home until seven o' clock from the office.

"So it's true. Antonella had killed someone named Anne." said Kevin, sitting down next to Genie.

Genie put the empty glass on the table and said-

"Yes, Rose said 'she killed my Anne', remember. And Antonella wrote 'I killed my Anne'..."

"I don't think Anne was a bird or an animal"

"Yeah, Rose won't cry like that because someone had killed her pet."

"But she looked mad, sometimes."

"That's true. Minaz knew something. Maria and Merina knew something and-"

"And Antonella knew everything." said Kevin seriously. Genie sighed and looked at the clock hanging on the blue painted wall. It was six o' clock.

"Kevin, I want a phone" said Genie still looking at the clock.

"What?"

"A phone" she repeated looking at him.

"Oh, yeah" He got to his feet and went to his room. After a minute, he came with a mobile phone in his hands. He handed it to her. She dialled her mother's number.

"Hello, Mum.."

"Yeah Genie."

"I will be in Kevin's house till eight o' clock. I have to help him with our home works."

"Ok, Bye."

"Bye" Genie did cut the phone and looked at him.

"We must ask Merina about the whole thing" suggested Kevin.

"But, I don't think it would be wise to tell her all these secrets..." hearing this, Kevin looked at her questioningly.

"First, you saw a sobbing girl. And then, we found a trapdoor. We met Maria there. Then we became friends with the strange girl named Rose Ginch. She told us many strange things. Then we met Minaz... oh, we can't tell her all these now. We have to investigate. And Maria told us don't say anything to anyone, remember? If Merina had told Maria that we had said everything to her... and... but..but..oh, it's all confusing!" Genie said, very puzzled.

"I think, we can connect your strange feeling and Antonella's murder to all these things..." said Kevin.

"WOOH!" Genie jumped up in a sudden thought of something. Kevin gazed at her.

"LEDA!" squealed Genie.

A look of great terror came to his face.

"WHERE SHE IS? " Genie squeaked.

"I - I - OH MY GOD - I - I -" Kevin sat there, unable to say anymore.

"K - Kevin, usually, she meets you from a little bit near to your house, am I right? " Genie asked him, sitting near him and putting an arm on his shoulder rapidly. He was sitting with his face buried in his hands and he nodded, still his face buried in his hands.

"Kevin, and -" Genie stopped there, having a doubt that if Kevin was weeping silently.

"Kevin? " she said in a low and caring voice. But there was no answer.

"Kevin? Are you OK? Kevin? Kevin? " Genie said, shaking him softly with her hands. Kevin gave a sob.

"Hey! Kevin? " she moved his fingers and now she can see his face and of course! He was weeping.

"Oh, Kevin... " she shook him and then he lost the control of himself and he started crying more loudly.

"Kevin, don't be so discouraged... have strength... come on... " Genie said in a sisterly voice.

Kevin wiped his face and looked at her.

"Everyday - you kn - know her school is beyond this - this house a - and - and I has the key and ev - everyday, she waits f - f - for me in front of the house - and - and - and - a - gg - ggh -" his uncontrollable sobs killed his words and she patted on his shoulder. Genie looked around and stood up, determined.

"Come on! " she said and he stopped sobbing and looked up at her. "Come on! " she pulled him by the arms. He wiped his tears away, when got to his feet. He looked into her eyes and she looked back into his eyes. It was a silent talk with eyes. Then they nodded at each other and rushed out of the house.

They got to the veranda. Genie climbed down and waited for him. Kevin locked the door and pushed the key into his pocket, hurrying down to her. They walked swiftly, watching all around them. Then they heard a sound and looked up. It was a little blue bird chirping on a tree. Genie saw something green near it. It would be the leaves. They took their eyes off the tree, knowing that it was not important to them, now.

" Hey! " Genie stopped there. What was the green thing? It shouldn't be the leaves. The leaves of that tree were dark green and the green she saw was a sort of very bright, glittering green.

" What is it? " Kevin who was still walking without knowing that Genie had stopped there, stopped and looked back at her. Genie said nothing but looked quickly at the tree. Of course, there was something bright, glittering green... it was a cloth... it was a small frock... and there were little legs and hands visible in the large group of the leaves. It was - it was -

" LEDA! LEDA! " Genie cried. Kevin gazed at her. She stared at the tree. There was a little girl standing on the highest branch of the tree. The tree was so tall and slippery and Leda's position was really dangerous. Genie was unable to see her face, because it was hidden in the green leaves.

Leda's little white hands were clutched tightly around the wood and unbelievably, they were not shuddering a little. They were bravely still.

Genie heard her own heart thumping loudly. She ran swiftly towards the tree and she heard Kevin doing the same, behind her. She got right under the tree and she started to climb without wasting a moment. Kevin was right behind her. The two of them grew panicky as they were climbing and climbing as fast as they could, but little Leda was still far away. Leda was standing still as though she was not seeing or hearing her brother and his best friend coming towards her. Then suddenly she looked down. Genie and Kevin froze. Leda's small face was too white and pale. And her green eyes were burning strangely, in the same way the girl called Rose Ginch's eyes burned. Leda stared at the two of them with burning eyes.

Leda stepped forward. Her burning eyes were still fixed on Genie and Kevin. Leda moved again, still staring at them. Her hands loosened and slowly, they came down, and now she was standing on the tall, slippery tree, without gripping anywhere with her hands. And she moved and moved. Now she was on the edge of the branch, and if she took one more step, she will fall down. She stood still for one second. And then her foot began to move slowly. She was going to take one more step... and - and - Genie's heart sank.

One second! Without a warning, Genie sped up. She was running up through the dangerously slippery branches... and then she found herself standing on the highest branch of the tree, and one of her arms were holding Leda. Leda was standing with her face hidden in Genie's chest.

" Leda, Leda. " She whispered and Leda looked up. Her face was ordinary again and her eyes were not burning anymore. She nodded at something only she knew.

Kevin climbed onto the branch and hugged Leda. Then they all climbed down. Kevin and Genie were holding the little hands of Leda when they were climbing down. When they reached down, Genie and Kevin stood face to face with Leda. Her eyes suddenly became dreamy. Kevin and Genie looked at each other. Then Genie looked at Leda, surprised.

" How did you get on the tree? Why did you climb onto it? " It was Kevin who broke the silence. Leda made no answer and Kevin repeated the same questions. Then a strange glittery flash appeared in Leda's eyes. And without a warning, she fainted.Genie and Kevin ran towards her and sat near her, rapidly. They shook her face again and again, but she did not open her eyes.

" Leda! "

" Leda! "

Kevin took her in his arms and looked at her face, brotherly. Her face exactly looked like a tired, closed Lotus which was shining energetically, four minutes ago.

They took her into the house, and laid her comfortably on her soft bed. Genie sat beside her. Kevin opened the water jeg on the tiny table near the bed. He held it upside down with his right hand, and the water flowed into his left hand. He was too quick or his hand was trembling that the waterdrops fell all over the floor. Kevin placed the jeg back on the table and ran towards Leda. He shook his hand right up to her face and her face became wet with waterdrops that fell from his hand.

A sign of disturbance came to her face and slowly, she opened her eyes. She looked at Genie and then, she burst into tears.

"Leda! What's happening to you! "

Genie and Kevin became puzzled and tensed. They laid their hands on Leda's small, shivering shoulders. She tried to sit up. They helped her and she sat up on the bed. She continued to sob. Genie moved more close to Leda. A strange glittery flash appeared in Genie's eyes.

Leda said, her eyes becoming dreamy : " I'm not well. Since the previous week, I began to feel something strange. And that strange feeling was growing so wild, and today, I couldn't controll myself, and a strange desire made me climb that tree. I don't know... a really strange feeling... a feeling like an - an -"

"An ocean roaring inside you. A feeling like an ocean roaring inside you, isn't it? " Genie said. Leda became so surprised and she stared at Genie, her eyes filled with wonder. " Is there anything about a tiger? " Genie asked.

"Of course, there is! One week ago, my dearest friend gifted me a picture. It was so beautiful. A really lovely picture of a tiger. When I looked at it, that wild feeling came. I always had that feeling when I thought about a tiger or saw a tiger. It's not a new thing to me. I kept that picture with me wherever I went. And the feeling began to grow madly. And all these things happened. " Leda finished thoughtfully.

" Show me that picture, " said Genie, detectively. Leda pushed one of her hands into her pocket and pulled out a small picture. She handed it to Genie. Genie took it and began to examine it. It was a wonderful picture of a huge tiger, drinking water from a clear stream, in the middle of a forest.

An ocean started to roar inside Genie.

" You said your dearest friend gifted this picture to you, didn't you? " Genie asked, seriously. Leda nodded. " Who was it? "

" Merina. She gave me this, " answered Leda. Genie and Kevin looked at each other.

" Merina Yumia? "

" Yes. She is in your grade, right? And I really like her.

Her house stood behind my school and we meets every evening," Leda said, a gladness appearing in her face at sound of Merina's name.

Kevin said : " Come on, Genie, we are wasting our time. We should go back to our works and leave Leda to take rest."

Genie and Kevin were now sitting back in the living room.

" All these things are connected, " said Genie thoughtfully. " I mean - just think - I had a strange feeling about tigers. And there's a trapdoor. There's a girl called Rose Ginch who knows so many details about me and you. And that letter. The secret between Maria and Rose. The secret between Merina and Antonella. And Leda's feeling which is same as mine. And the friendship between Leda and

Merina. And -"

" It's too difficult, " said Kevin, puzzled.

" Of course, it is... but we have to find it... " Genie was so interested.

Then a woman with red hair and green eyes entered the living room through the open door. Then came a tall, handsome man with brown hair, just behind her. They were Mrs and Mr Notts, the parents of Kevin and Leda. They saw Genie and Kevin sitting on the armchairs and they smiled at them, a little surprised to see Genie. She and Kevin stood up and smiled at them.

"Hello, I believe that you are my son's friend, and am I right? " Mr Notts said, looking at Genie with a pleasant face.

"Oh, yeah... " said Genie, trying to smile. She was still weak because of the adventures she had with Kevin, one hour ago.

"Dad, this is Genie, my best friend, " said Kevin.

"Aha, so this is the smart Genie. Kevin always kept saying about you. 'Genie did this, Genie did that...' And me and

John knew you are kevin's bestie, " said Mrs Notts, smiling so warmly.

" Ahh... glad to meet you. " Mr Notts held out his right hand. " Johnson." He said his name. Genie shook his hand.

CHAPTER THREE
ARASENMOSIS

Then she heard someone knocking at the door. Genie's heart sank. A tiger is sleeping in her bed... she got up and walked to the door.

" Wh - who's there? " she asked in a shaky voice.

" It's me, your mum. Open the door. " said the soft voice from outside.

" What is it? " asked Genie.

" Kevin is here to meet you" said her mother.

" Tell him to come here. " said Genie. And her mother's footsteps walked away. She was relieved. And then she heard someone's footsteps coming. She was sure it was Kevin.

" Genie? " came Kevin's voice.

" Kevin, is there someone with you? " asked Genie in a low voice.

" N - no. " answered Kevin.

Genie opened the door and pulled Kevin in swiftly and immediately locked the door. Kevin tried to shriek at sight of Tigo, by Genie clapped her hand to his mouth, rapidly.

" Be silent. " she whispered and took her hands back.

Kevin looked really panicky. He stared at Tigo.

Tigo opened his eyes and tried to growl, but Genie shook her head and he became silent. She ran towards him and took the blanket from him. He sat up royally and stretched his legs. Genie patted on his back in a friendly way and said:

" Good morning, Tigo. "

Kevin became more more white and pale and he said:

" T - T - Tigo? "

" Of course, Tigo. " said Genie coolly.

" That tiger in Littlegreen Zoo? " asked Kevin, shivering. Genie nodded, smiling.

" Oh, my Go - " Kevin fell down, faintly, before he could complete the sentence.

Genie ran towards him. He layed on the floor, his eyes closed.

" Kevin! Kevin! " Genie shook him, but he was fainted. She ran to the wash-basin and took a hand ful of water and poured it on his face. Then he opened his eyes and stared at Genie and jumped to his feet and gave a loud cry:

" OH MY GOD! " and fell down, fainted again.

" Is there any problem? " asked Genie's mum from outside the room, who came running, hearing the cry.

" No, Mum. Kevin saw a snake under my bed. " Genie lied.

" WHAT? A SNAKE? " cried Rachel Razi, her mother. Genie felt that she had done something stupid. She had to lie to make her mum no panicky, but now her mum had became so panicky because of her lie.

" No need to worry, mum. It was just one of my toys. You know, that snake-toy I bought saying it looks so realistic? " said Genie.

" Oh, " said her mother, relieved and walked away.

Genie turned to Kevin. He had recovered from the shock

and was sitting on the floor, wheezing.

" Kevin, come on. " said Genie and she helped him to stand up. She told him to sit on the bed, but he refused because there was Tigo, sitting on the bed.

" Don't be scared. Look, you are not scared of Sam, are you? " asked Genie and Kevin shook his head.

" You are not scared of Jane, are you? "

" No. "

" Why? "

" They are your pets. "

" Tigo is my pet, too. "

" What? "

" Kevin, sit down, let me explain everything. " said Genie and at last, Kevin sat down on the bed. Genie told him everything that happened after she had left his house, yesterday.

He sat there, thunderstruck, after hearing everything. Genie sat next to him. She stood up, silently. Sam and Jane came to Kevin's lap, but he ignored them. Genie walked to the bathroom, leaving Kevin with his shock.

After brushing her teeth, Genie came back and sat near him. He looked at her.

" Don't be so panicked. We can complete this adventures. Believe me. " said Genie, kindly and Kevin nodded and tried to smile. Someone knocked at the door and then came Rachel's voice:

" Genie, Kevin, come. Have breakfast. "

" We are coming, Mum " said Genie.

The footsteps went away. Genie led Tigo to the large box, under the cupboard. She opened it. It was full of teddy-bears. Genie began to move all the teddy-bears to the cupboard and Kevin came to help her. They emptied the box and put it to under the bed. Genie layed a soft blanket in the box and put a big pillow in it. And the box was now, hidden under the bed.

"Tigo, get in. " said Genie. Tigo stepped into the box and layed in it. No one can see him, now. If anyone looked at under the bed, they could only see only a small part of the box.

" Come on. " said Genie to Kevin.

" Sam, Jane, aren't you coming? " she asked and the pup and the cat ran to her feet.

" Hello. " Kevin smiled and took Jane in his arms. Jane was his favourite and he was Jane's favourite. Sam looked at Genie, hopefully. A naughty smile appeared on Genie's lips and she bent down and took the little pup in her hands. Sam looked at Jane with great triumph. Jane blinked at him and turned her head away from him and began to rub her furry head on Kevin's fingers, lazily.

Before opening the door, Genie looked back and made sure that everything was OK, she turned to the door again and opened it. They walked to the dining room. There was Rachel waiting for them in a chair.

" Genie, are you alright? " she asked. Genie nodded.

" She was faint, yesterday. " said Rachel, looking at Kevin.

" Ah, she told me. " he said.

" Kevin, did you eat the breakfast? " she asked.

" Er - no, " he said, " I ran to here, hearing that she was ill" Rachel smiled and rose. She walked to the kitchen.

" Who told you, I was ill? " asked Genie.

" No one told me. " Kevin whispered.

" Then? " Genie raised her eyebrows.

"I heard dad talking to mum. I will explain everything to you after breakfast" he said, seeing Rachel coming out of the kitchen with some dishes in her hands.

Rachel placed the dishes on the dining table. Genie and Kevin put Sam and Jane down and went to wash their hands. After a silent breakfast, they were walking back to Genie's room.

" Mum, it's already late, won't you go to the cafe? " called Genie.

" No, I'm not going. Your father said I would stay here and take care of you. Today, Manha would look after the cafe. " answered Rachel from the living room. She was sitting there with a fat book in her hands.

Genie pushed the door open and she went in with Kevin. They locked it from inside. Tigo came out of the box, as Genie told him to do so. Genie and Kevin sat on the bed, face to face and Tigo sat on her feet.

" Now, tell me everything" said Genie.

" Yesterday, at night, my dad came back home. He was worried and when he got to home, I asked him what happened. He said nothing. He said to Mum to follow him and they went into their room and locked the door. There was a serious talk between them. I stood in front of the door, spying. But they were talking in a very low voice and I could hear nothing. Once, Dad's voice raised up to normal size and I heard that you were ill. Then mum said shhh and Dad's voice lowered again into a whisper. I went to my room and slept. And today morning, I woke up and then I remembered about you. So I said that I need to see you and before eating breakfast, I came here. "

As Kevin finished, a serious problem poked up in Genie's head.

" Kevin, we must go. " she said.

" Come in, let's go, hide Tigo in the box, " said Kevin, getting to his feet.

" We must go with Tigo. " Genie said.

" But, how - "

" We will go. " said Genie sharply.

" I will be back in two minutes. Wait till then. " she said and stood up. She went to the table and took her drawing book. She got out of the room. Rachel was sitting in the living room, her eyes fixed on the fat book which was laying open in her lap. Genie walked to her parents' room, silently. When she got there, she hid the drawing book in a cupboard. Then she came to the living room.

" What is it, Genie? " she asked looking at Genie.

" Can you give me my drawing book? " Genie asked.

" It's there on your table. " said Rachel, simply.

" I searched for it, but it wasn't there. " said Genie, acting innocently.

Rachel got to her feet and walked to Genie's room.

" No, mum! It's not there! Search for it in your room! " cried Genie. Rachel threw a doubtful look at Genie. Then she walked to her own room.

When she had got out of sight, Genie ran to her own room.

" Come on, come on. " she muttered.

" But - " Kevin was afraid.

" Come on! " she hissed. He stood up and walked to the door with Tigo.

" Hurry up... " hissed Genie. The three ran out of the house. Genie stopped at the veranda and said.

" Run! Run! " Kevin and Tigo ran away and were out of sight. At that moment, Rachel came out with the drawing book in her hands.

" Here you are! Where are you going? " she asked, giving the book to Genie.

" I'm going to Kevin's house. " answered Genie. Rachel gave a confused look.

" He said I could draw with him in his house. " Genie lied.

" Then, where is he? "

" He went to home. I am going... " said Genie, hurriedly, fearing that her Mum would ask more questions.

Genie ran away. She reached the grassy land, on which Kevin was standing with Tigo.

" How you did it? " it was Kevin, who asked so.

" I hid my drawing book in my mum's room and then I told her my drawing book is missing and she went to search for it. That was the time, when you and Tigo ran away. Then Mum found the book and gave me. I told her I an going to draw some pictures in it, at your house and came here" Genie explained.

" You are so clever. " said Kevin, amazed.

" Oh, everybody says so! " said Genie, trying to hide a proud smile. Tigo gave a growl.

" Come, " Genie was too excited and hurried. They walked through the wet path with the signs of the rain from the previous night. Genie and Kevin were careful to keep the tiger away from the people. But they were lucky, there were no passers-by on the path. There was a turning of the path. They can't see what's coming from beyond the turning. Then they heard some footsteps coming in their direction from beyond the turning. They stopped, alarmed. Genie and Kevin exchanged some panicked looks. They looked around for a place to hide Tigo, but there was nothing like what they were looking for.

Genie and Kevin grew more more worried and they tried to hide the tiger behind them, but they were too late. A man appeared in front of them from beyond the turning. It was a handsome man with a well-shaped nose and deep blue eyes. His hair was thick and black and long. Genie and Kevin stopped dead at sight of him. It was Alfred Minaz.

" Aha! A tiger! " he said with a short smile.

" Whose tiger is this? " asked Minaz. Kevin tried to say " we don't know " But Genie said sharply before he could utter a word: " Mine! "

Kevin looked at her, scared.

" So you are a Tiger-Girl, aren't you? " said Minaz.

" Of course, I am! " said Genie, boldly. Minaz nodded with a thoughtful smile.

" Littlegreen Zoo... hmm... Littlegreen Zoo... " he muttered. Then he passed them, humming a mysterious tune.

" Genie, don't be so stupid. " snapped Kevin.

" He understood everything. We know him. He is not so nice. And you had told him everything. He would throw us into serious troubles," he snapped hotly. Genie looked at him. Her look was so sharp and Kevin had to look away. Genie continued that sharp look and Kevin did not dare to look at her till she had looked away.

They had a silent walk and got to the trapdoor in the bush. Genie got into the bush and she knocked at the trapdoor. She gave a knock and waited. Then the trapdoor opened. Genie was waiting for Rose, but without a warning, a big tigress jumped out.

" Uhh! " Genie fell back.

" Oh, hi. " said Rose, climbing out of the trapdoor.

" Toma, my tigress. " she said, looking at the tigress.

" Hmm. " Genie nodded, sitting up.

Kevin came there and stopped dead at sight of Toma. Tigo ran forward to Toma.

" Don't be scared. It's my tigress. Toma. She is only a poor creature. " said Rose, smiling and Kevin looked at Genie and Genie nodded. Toma and Tigo started rubbing their heads together.

" I think, they were great friends back in the forest. And then the people working for the zoo caught them and separated them. And now, they are together again and see how happy they are. " Rose said with a kind smile at the tiger and the tigress.

"I have a doubt. " said Kevin.

" What is it? " asked Genie and Rose, together.

" Am I a Tiger-Boy? " Kevin asked. Genie and Rose looked at each other.

" Ahem, ahem! " Rose made a fake cough and Kevin and Genie looked at her.

" Kevin, do you have a strange, wild feeling when you talk or think about tigers? " asked Rose. Kevin thought for a moment.

" What kind of feeling, you mean? " he asked.

" Er - like a - a - like an ocean roaring inside you. " explained Genie. Kevin remained thoughtful and then he shook his head and said:

" No. "

" So, you are not a Tiger-Boy. " said Rose, simply.

" Hoooo... " said Kevin, relieved.

" I am lucky. " he said.

" What you mean? " asked Rose. Genie knew what he meant.

" I am lucky, that I am not a Tiger-Boy. " explained Kevin.

" Hey, silly boy, being a Tiger-Boy or a Tiger-Girl is not an unlucky thing. It is a wonderful, good and - " Genie threw a warning look at Rose and Rose stopped there.

Kevin bowed his head down.

" Kevin, cheer up. There are so many things to be happy at. Being a Tiger-Boy or a Tiger-Girl is not a devoted thing. Being an ordinary human being is not a shameful thing. That's not two things we can compare with each other. Got it?" said Genie, sisterly. Kevin did not look up.

" Oh, you stupid boy, look at the parrots and peacocks.

The peacocks are so beautiful and looks wonderful. The parrots can fly in the sky. But, I don't think that any peacock would be sad at the fact that the parrots can fly but he can't, and any parrot would be sad at the fact that the peacocks do look wonderful but he don't. And -"

" Oh, Genie, I am seeing you being a very serious old professor for the first time in my life" said Kevin, with a funny smile and Rose broke into laughter.

Genie looked from Kevin to Rose and then again at Kevin. The two of them were laughing together like they had just heard the bestest joke in the world and Genie seemed furious.

She ran towards Kevin and Rose and tried to pull their hair. Kevin ran away, laughing, but Rose was still there and Genie pulled her hair and she screamed with laughter and Kevin began to laugh harder. Rose got out of Genie's reach and she panted, looking at Genie. Genie let out a roar of laughter and Rose jumped towards her. But Genie was keen than her and she, Genie ran away. Rose chased her, but she did not catch her and she sat back on the grass, tired. Kevin was watching all these with a funny expression on his face. Rose sat near him. She was panting more heavily. Genie was not tired and she came back to them and sat next to Rose and started laughing loudly with Kevin.

Finally, Kevin and Genie had stopped laughing and Rose had got her breathe back, Rose said:

" I've got something to tell you. "

Everybody including Tigo and Toma wore a serious expression on their faces.

" Genie, I want you in presence of Arasenmosis, today, " said Rose and Genie and Kevin exchanged a puzzled look.

" Er - sorry? " said Genie, her eyes narrowing.

" I want you in presence of Arasenmosis. " repeated Rose, seriously.

" Arase - what? " said Genie.

" Arasenmosis. "

" Arasenmo... "

" Ara - sen - mosis. " said Rose, slowly and clearly.

" Arasenmosis. " said Genie thougtfully.

" Yeah, Arasenmosis. " Rose nodded.

" Arasenmosis. " Genie repeated triumphantly.

" Yes, that's it. Arasenmosis. " said Rose, knowingly.

" Arasenmosis. Arasenmosis. Arasenmosis. Arazzen-mozziz. " said Genie.

" Not Arazzenmoz -" Rose began to correct, but then Kevin, who was watching all these silently, burst out:

" Could you drop this Arasenmosis thing off and say what you was going to say? "

Genie and Rose looked at each other.

" I think Kevin's right. Well, you must say what you was going to say... " Genie said, looking at Rose.

" Yeah, " said Rose, " I want you in presence of Aras -"

" Who's Arasenmosis? " asked Genie.

" He's a tree. " answered Rose.

" A tree? " repeated Genie and Kevin together.

" Yep. A tree. And he's not an ordinary tree. He's - he's -"

" Magical? " said Genie eagerly.

" Could you please keep silent till I finish? " said Rose, very very elderly.

" Of course, I would. You continue. " said Genie, nodding calmly.

" So, Arasenmosis is the leader of the Tiger-Girls and Tiger-Boys all over the world. He can talk. And so, you are a Tiger-Girl and now you had found your tiger and it would be nice if you come to meet him. And you know, I had found my tigress, just like you, so, I have got to go to him already, and you can come with me. " Rose finished and Genie's eyes widened with eagerness and wonder.

Kevin was sitting, too bored, that Rose was completely ignoring him and was talking to Genie, as though there was no Kevin near them.

" Ooohhh... " Genie held her right hand out and rubbed her fingers on the elbow of his arm in great excitement.

" It would be wonderful... " she muttered.

" Oh, Kevin, we are going to visit a talking tree! " she said, looking at Kevin, her voice rising enthusiastically.

" No! " cried Rose. Genie and Kevin looked at her with narrowed eyes.

" We can't take him with us! He is not one of us! " said Rose, still ignoring Kevin.

" What you mean? He is one of us! " said Genie, starting to feel furious.

" He is not a Tiger-Boy! We can't take him with us! We can't reveale our secrets to him! "

" Rose, don't be so selfish. " Genie said angrily.

" We can't reveale our secrets to him! We must not reveale our secrets to him! And we are not going to reveale any of our secrets to him! " commanded Rose.

Genie looked at Kevin. He was staring from her at Rose and then back at her and again at Rose. His face was reddening. Genie knew what he was feeling and she was getting ready to console him. But before she could utter a word, he stood up and said hotly:

" You could stay here, discussing your secrets with her. And I have nothing to do with the secrets of you and her and I am leaving. " Kevin managed to ignore Rose completly, in the same way in which she ignored him.

" Kevin, don't be so silly. Don't mind what this foolish girl is saying. I would take you with me. And -"

" Oh, your kindness! AND I DON'T WANT IT! I AM LEAVING. YOU STAY HERE WITH YOUR AND HER SECRET. Goodbye. " Kevin shouted, stopping Genie in midsentence. Genie began to get angry at him.

" FINE! " she shouted back.

Kevin walked away fastly, leaving Genie breathing furiously, Rose smiling in a misty way, Tigo and Toma looking from him at Genie, confused. Rose waited till he vanished from sight and then she opened her mouth and said coolly:

" Well, shall we go? "

Genie smiled at Rose, now feeling perfectly friendly to her.

" Er - on which place Arasenmosis stand? If it's far away -" Genie began, but then Rose said:

" Not too far... just beyond those... " Genie felt her insides trembling as Rose was pointing at the white clouds in the blue sky.

" What? You're kidding. " said Genie.

"I'm not" said Rode, smiling.

" Do just like I do. " said Rose and she beckoned Toma towards her. Rose rubbed her fingers on the forehead of the tigress for ten times and then rubbed the very edge of the tail of Toma for ten times, too. Genie watched this carefully and she walked towards Tigo. She rubbed her own finger's on Tigo's forehead and tail for ten times.

Genie saw a pair of shiny white wings appearing on the back of Rose. And there came a pair of white wings on the back of Toma, too.

" How wondeful... " Genie whispered. She became more amazed to see a pair of bright glittery blue wings appearing on the back of Tigo.

" Wow... " Genie ran her fingers through those beautiful wings.

" Ha! Look at your own back! " said Rose coolly.

" What? " Genie turned her arms to examine her own back. She became so excited than ever when she touched two bright glittery wings on her back.

" UNBELIEVABLE! " she cried.

" OK, but don't yell. " said Rose in a low voice. She was smiling in a lovely way. Genie loved it so much and she was ready to hug Rose at the very moment. Wings! Real wings!

" Come on! " said Rose and she rose to the air with her wings fluttering. Toma took off, too. Genie took a deep breath and jumped up into the air and she did not fall back to the ground. She stayed in the fresh morning air. Tigo was doing the same as Toma.

" What if someone see us? " said Genie looking at Rose.

" We are invisible to the people except Tiger-Girls and Tiger-Boys" said Rose simply. Genie stared at her, thunder-struck.

" What? " said Genie, "So, my parents are not Tiger-People and so, you mean they can't see me anymore? "

" The people who are not Tiger-People can't see us only when we are in the air on our wings. " said Rose shortly.

Genie sighed with great relief.

" Come, let's go. " said Rose and she flew high with Tigo and Toma.

" Oh, yeah, " said Genie, flying high to catch up with them.

They flew and flew... the cool and fresh air was running through her hair and Genie was enjoying it, like she enjoys the air running through her hair, when she travels, sitting on the window seat.

They flew through a large pack of clouds. Flying through

the clouds was like flying through some warm white spongy smoke. Genie closed her eyes and flew through the spongy warm smoke. And at last, the warmth of those spongy smoke and she guessed that they had passed the clouds and got beyond them.

Genie opened her eyes, slowly. She saw a hill. A small green hill in the air. It was covered with clouds and it was so lovely. How fascinating! A hill in the sky. A big tree was there at top of the hill.

They flew for some minutes and then landed on top of the hill. The ground was covered with soft green grasses and yellow leaves that had fallen from the tree. The tree stood with its countless strong branches and green leaves. There were two small eyes and a nose and lips with a warm smile on its wood.

" Good morning, Arasenmosis. " said Rose.

" Good morning, M - ah - Rossie. " said Arasenmosis brightly.

" Rossie, I hope that tigress is Toma and you had rescued her from the zoo, last night. " said the tree.

" Of course. You're right. And I'm happy. " said Rose gladly.

Then, the smile on her face faded. A sad shadow came into her eyes.

" Just happy about Toma, " she sighed, " I'm still trapped in the memories of her... "

Genie could not think whom Rose was talking sadly about at once. Then, she remembered: Rose was talking about Anne.

" Still being sad about Anne? " said Arasenmosis.

" How could I be glad about her? How could I forget her? How -"

" OK, OK, enough. I know it. " said Arasenmosis, looking alarmed at sight of Rose's eyes starting to sparkle with tears. Genie was sure that Arasenmosis wanted to change the topic, but she did not want to. She do not want to see Rose weeping, but she do want to hear more about Anne.

" Who is this pretty girl? " asked Arasenmosis.

" Oh, this, this's my friend Genie. You know, Genie Razi. " Rose said, looking at Genie.

" Oh, I know. Genie. That girl in -"

" NO! " warned Rose, stopping Arasenmosis at midsetnence.

" What is it? " asked Genie, looking from Rose to Arasenmosis.

" Nothing. Oh, well, hello, Genie. " Arasenmosis smiled at her.

" Hello. " said Genie gently.

" Is this Tigo? " he asked, pointing the thinnest branch of his at the tiger.

" Yeah, this's Tigo. I rescued him from the zoo last night with Rose. " said Genie. " How d'you know? "

" Rossie told me. " said Arasenmosis, simply.

" Come on. Have a fruit. " said Arasenmosis. Genie did not realise what he meant for a moment. Then she saw tiny gentle red fruits hanging on the branches of Arasenmosis.

She and Rose walked to get closer to the tree and then plucked out severel ripen fruits from the lowest branches.

Genie looked at the shining red fruits in her hands. She examined it carefully, while Rose was pushing all of the fruits she had into her mouth at one time and enjoying those fruits with her eyes closed. Genie had never seen any kind of fruits like this before. They were not Apples. Not Cherries. So, Genie continued to examine them carefully.

" Hey, tghnff... " Rose swallowed the fruits and then said clearly:

" Hey, they're not poisonous fruits. Eat them."

Genie looked at Rose and then looked back at the fruits. Then she decided to stop examining and put one of the fruits into her mouth. At first no taste... then she made a tiny hole at top of the fruit... there came really unbelievably tasty juice out of it... Genie gulped down the sweet juice.

" How's it? " asked Rose, smiling.

" Yummy... " whispered Genie, now chewing the fruit and enjoying the taste of it, her eyes closed. Rose and Arasenmosis laughed out. Genie ate the all fruits in her hand and then looked up at Arasenmosis.

" Hee, hee, hee! " Arasenmosis laughed and beckoned her towards him with his ranches.

Genie walked to him. As she got nearer, the tree whispered:

" Take some more, if you like. "

Genie looked at him and then both of them broke into laughter at the same time. Rose joined them in laughing as though she knew what they were laughing at.

" What? " Genie asked her.

" Hmm? " Rose looked at her.

" What you are laughing at? " Genie asked.

" I am laughing at what you and Arasenmosis are laughing at. " Rose replied and Genie and Arasenmosis looked at each other with widened eyes.

" Anyway, leave it. Arasenmosis, I think you want to talk to Genie. " Rose said. Arasenmosis looked puzzled.

" Er - what I want to tell her? I don't think I told you I have to talk to her. " Arasenmosis said slowly, looking at Rose.

" Oh, Arasenmosis, your memory is getting bad. You told me you want to tell Genie something very important, remember? And that's why I took her with me or you. "

Rose said. Genie saw Rose's face being covered with sweat.

" No, Rossie. I never -" Arasenmosis began, but then Rose hissed :

" Arasenmosis... remember what I told you last time we met... "

Genie looked from Rose at Arasenmosis and back. Arasenmosis stared at Rose for a moment and then said as though he had just realized something very important :

" Oh, oh... yes, I remember... " he looked at Genie.

" Yes, he I was wanting to talk to you, " he said, " I think my memory is getting really bad. " Arasenmosis added with a sideway glance at Rose.

" Well, Genie, d'you know Anne? " Arasenmosis asked, looking suddenly serious.

" Er - yeah I know... " Genie said, wondering what to say.

" OH NO! " Rose shrieked that made Genie jump.

" Calm down, Rossie. " Arasenmosis said softly.

" OH MY GOD...! WHAT CAN I DO...? " Rose screamed even more loudly and Genie gazed at Arasenmosis as though asking him what she could do now to calm Rose down.

" Keep silent, Rossie. " Said Arasenmosis.

" And, Genie, how do you know Anne? You see, she is not living in your neighbourhood nor studying in your school, " said Arasenmosis.

" Erm - at first, I didn't know Anne. But then I found out a few things. " Genie said slowly and Rose screamed and fell onto the grass. Genie ran towards her and helped her to sit up. Rose sobbed into her chest.

" Stop this nonsense" said Arasenmosis, now sounding angry. But Rose continued to weep and Genie looked up at Arasenmosis, tensed.

" Genie, leave her and come here" He said.

" But, Arasenmo -"

" DO WHAT I SAID! " Arasenmosis commanded and Genie stood up quickly. She gulped and walked towards Arasenmosis.

Genie stood in front of the tree. Then she threw a look at Rose with the corner of her eyes and saw Rose weeping into the green grass, laying on the ground. Arasenmosis cleared his throat loudly and Genie looked back at him.

" How do you know Anne? " Arasenmosis repeated.

" I don't know her directly. I just know that she is a dead girl and -"

" Oh! " Rose sat up rapidly and stared at her with her wide eyes alight.

Rose let out a sigh of relief and Arasenmosis smiled.

" Ther's a girl named Antonella Foa in my grade. One day, she gave a short letter to another girl named Merina Yumia. It fell out of Merina's pocket and I and Kevin - my best friend - took it and read it. In it, there was written that Antonella had killed Anne. " Genie said.

" Was there ' Yes... Antonella killed her Anne'?" Rose asked sharply.

" No, " Genie said quickly, " it was ' Yes... I killed my Anne... '

and, it was written by Antonella, so, 'I' might be Antonella. "

" Hmm... " Rose nodded, her eyes twinkling with tears.

" So, that's all? " Arasenmosis said.

" That's all. " Genei replied.

" Can you please tell me who is Anne? I'm sure you know everything about her. Tell me. " Genie said hopefully.

" So, Rossie, you may go. " Arasenmosis said as though Genie had not asked him to tell her about Anne. This ignorance made Genie disappointed.

" Come Genie. Let's go, " said Rose, who was now falsely cheerful. Genie had to do nothing but follow her.

" Goodbye, Arasenosis. " Rose said. Genie waved in farewell, too.

" Bye... see you again... " Arasenmosis called from behind as Genie and Rose reached the edge of the magical land in the sky.

They turned. Tigo and Toma were still playing happily.

" Oi... come on... " Rose called. The tigress looked up.

" Come, " said Genie. Toma and Tigo came near them. Genie looked at Rose. Rose stepped out of the edge of the land and then - fell down.

" ROSSSSE! " Genie screamed and ran and she slipped on the edge and fell out of the land, into the cool sky. She shrieked. She was falling down... and the wind was whipping her hair... then suddenly she felt something supporting her. Yes, she was not falling anymore. She was balancing in mid air. Then she realized what was supporting her - wings.

She looked down. Rose was flying up towards her. When Rose came face to face with her, she said :

" You got scared, didn't you? "

" I thought you fell down. " Genie said.

" I was just taking off. " Rose said simply.

Then they heard a sound from above and looked up. Tigo and Toma were flying down towards them. The two girls and their dear animals began their journey down.

" You said when we be winged, no one can see us. I mean no other people who are not Tiger-Girls or Tiger-Boys can see us. " Genie said.

" Yes, I said so and that's right" Rose said carelessly.

" So, how did Arasenmosis see us? " Genie asked her doubt.

Rose looked at her.

" You know, " said Genie, " Arasenmosis is not a Tiger-Man, is he? "

" He is a tree, " said Rose.

" So? " Genie raised her eyebrows.

" Only other human beings can't see us when we are winged. Trees and plants and animals and birds can see us, " answered Rose. Genie nodded.

Finally, they all landed on the earth into the green bush with four soft thuds.

" That was wonderful... " said Genie truthfully. Rose smiled.

Rose rubbed her fingers on Toma's forehead and the end of her tail for ten times and the wings on her back and Toma's back vanished, leaving some shiny white dust that melted into the air. Genie did the same and she felt her wings vanishing, too, while she watched Tigo's wings disappear.

A cool breeze was blowing and the sun shone more brightly. Clearly, it was noon.

" Genie, you must go back. " Rose said.

" Why? I'd love to stay here a little longer. " Genie said childishly.

" No. Your mother would be searching for you now. " Rose warned her.

" I told her I would be in Kevin's house. " Genie said simply.

" Yep. And what if your mother called Kevin's mother and asked if you were there? " Rose demanded.

" Oh, that's right. " Genie said quickly, alarmed.

" I would go... " she sighed.

" Come on, let's go. " Genie said, looking at Tigo, who was playing with Toma. Tigo looked up and by then, Toma got to her feet swiftly, who was pinned to the earth by Tigo's strong paws.

" Hey! Tigo! " Genie said as though she just remembered something very important. Genie looked at Rose. Rose raised her eyebrows.

" How can I take Tigo into my house? Surely, Mum would be there in the varandah, waiting for me. " Genie said.

" Tigo will stay here with me and Toma, " Rose said cool-ly.

" Oh, I would - I would - miss him, " said Genie.

" Dont be so childish. Go. " Rose said seriously and Genie bent down and kissed her tiger on the forehead.

" Bye. " Genie said. And she stepped out of the bush. She heard Tigo's groans from behind her. She walked sadly. She walked as fast as she could. At last, she got in front of her house. Her Mum was sitting on a chair in the varandah as she expected.

" Ah, here you are. I was waiting for you. Come and have some lunch. " Rachel said, getting to her feet.

" Where's your drawing book? " she asked.

Genie froze for a moment. She gulped. Sweat appeared on her face.

" Er - I - I - I forgot to take it back from Kevin's house " Genie lied, looking at the carpet.

" Oh, that's fine. Come in, come in " Rachel said kindly. Genie started to step onto the varandah and Rachel turned to get into the house. Genie stopped and let out a sign of relief. Rachel stopped at the doorway and turned.

" Hurry... " she said. Genie got into the house.

CHAPTER FOUR

MERINA'S DIARY

A day passed. Genie felt so dull when she stepped into the classroom. She put her bag down and looked around for Kevin, as usual. He was playing with Georgina. Genie opened her mouth to call his name, cheerfully. But then she remembered that they were on a fight. She closed her mouth immediately. She felt very very angry towards Georgina, for no reoson. Georgina was playing with Kevin, happily and her long blond hair was shaking side to side. Genie turned her face away from the pair of them.

She sat down in her seat. She did not know what to do. She pulled her Mathematics note book out of her bag. She opened the book and took the last page. The last page of her Mathematics note book was a wide gallery of her emotions. There, she writes her thoughts, feelings, plans and draws small pictures to express her feelings and all those stuff filled the page. To others, the page looked like a page filled with so many alphabets and pictures and they can't read or recognise anything out of it, but Genie can. And she was not ready to take a new page.

Genie drew a very angry red face. Then she wrote 'Georgina' and drew large cuts all over the name furiously. Then she did the same to Kevin's name, too.

Genie could not stop herself from throwing sideway glances at Kevin and Georgina. Once, Georgina's eyes met hers. Genie wore a most angry expression on the face and stared at Georgina, as sharp as she could that her eyes started watering. Georgina smiled at Genie and she looked a little surprised to see that Genie did not smile back.

" Hey, Gennie. Hello! " Georgina called gently. Kevin looked at Genie and his smile vanished. Genie said nothing.

" Hey, why are you so serious? " Georgina walked towards Genie.

" Why are you so serious, Gennie? " Georgina repeated.

" That's none of your business. " Genie said sharply and she got satisfied seeing Georgina's bright smile vanishing.

" Gennie? " Georgina said, her eyes narrowed.

" Oh, yeah? " Genie said. Georgina got her smile back and said:

" Hey, don't act so angry, girl. It don't match to you. Your usual happy expression is perfect match to you. Anyway, why an angry expression?"

Genie burst out.

" I TOLD YOU THAT IS NONE OF YOUR BUSINESS! " Genie shouted at Georgina. Everybody looked at the pair of them. Kevin came hurrying to them.

" Why are you shouting at me? " Georgina asked in a small, shocked voice.

" YOU HAVE NOTHING TO DO WITH IT! DON'T ACT LIKE SO SMART, " Genie yelled angrily, " AND -"

" And I am sorry. " Kevin said. Genie stopped suddenly and stared at Kevin. Georgina, too was gazing at him. Everyone's eyes were fixed upon him.

" For what? " Genie heard herself asking and when she heard it, she thought that she knew for what Kevin was sorry.

" You know. " Kevin said. Genie saw a small smile appearing on his lips, slowly. Before she could stop herself, a smile began to appear on her own lips. When she realized it, it was too late. And she allowed the smile to be brighter.

" Friends again? " Genie said and held out a hand.

" Friends again. " Kevin shook it.

Beside them, Georgina gave an uncomfortable sigh and turned, shaking her head. She walked away, muttering something like "mad friends.."

" Oi! " Kevin called but Georgina did not look back.

" Georgina! " Genie called and this time, Georgina looked over her shoulders and then turned her face back, violently. Kevin and Genie looked at each other.

" Sorryeee... " Genie called cheerfully and Georgina looked back and smiled.

During the noon interval, Genie and Kevin were walking through their favourite path in the school compound. It was a very cool path. There were big trees standing on both sides of the path. The trees were all in the same height. They had bright green leaves. In the spring season, there would be countless pink flowers on the trees. The flowers had dark pink petals. The petals were so thin and it looked like many many pink threads pinned to the flower. Genie loved to pull the pink petals out and suck the sweet honey out of the naked flower.

This was the rainy season and the trees were covered in

green leaves. The path laid in the cool shades of them. The two friends walked chatting happily. Genie laughed gently at the jokes told by Kevin and Kevin enjoyed the tales told by Genie.

Then they saw Minaz, their least favourite teachers coming from the opposite direction. He smiled in a dirty way as usual. Genie and Kevin stopped, suddenly fallen silent and without any smile.

Genie's heart was pounding so hard. What would Minaz say? He knew she was a Tiger-Girl and she had got her tiger.

" Could you help me? " Minaz asked them. This was an unexpected question and Genie and Kevin looked at each other, completely puzzled.

" Did not you hear me? Could you help me Miss Razi and Mr Notts? " Minaz repeated coolly.

" Er - yeah. What can we do for you? Sir? " Genie asked quickly. Minaz gave a short, hollow laugh and said :

" Get the homework book of Merina Yumia for me. "

" Sir? "

" The Yumia girl is the only one who did not give her homework book to me. She told me she had forgotten or take it. " Minaz explained.

" I know it. I was in the classroom. " Genie said irritably.

" Of course, you were and I know Yumia was lying. And I know she had not done the homework. Now, she is playing with her friend in the ground and you two go to the classroom and open her bag and take the book and come back here. Go. Now" Minaz commanded.

Genie and Kevin turned and began to walk in the direction of their classroom.

" D'you know why Maria is not coming to school since the day of the Littlegreen Zoo trip? " Kevin broke the uncomfortable silence.

" Merina told me Maria had gone to another school, " replied Genie.

" Where? "

" Merina said Maria I staying in her Grandma's house. There is a school near that house and Maria is now studying there. "

" Why? She loves her own house and this school and I see no reason for her staying away. "

" I don't know. You know, Merina is a hub of secrets and she keeps her secrets as secrets... " Genie sighed deeply.

They got into the classroom and walked towards Merina's seat. Kevin bent down and opened her bag. Genie looked around, carelessly.

" Hey! " Kevin said unexpectedly and Genie looked at him. He was staring into the bag, his hands in the bag.

" What is it? " Genie asked nervously.

" This. " Kevin pulled out a large fat book out of the bag. It had shining black cover page.

" It looks like a diary. " Kevin said, excited.

" So? " Genie said dully.

" So, if we read this, we would find a few of the secrets of Merina. " Kevin said, grinning.

Genie stared at him.

" I don't think it is right to read someone's personal diary. " Genie said seriously.

" Oh, Genie, wait... " said Kevin who had already opened the diary and now turning the pages.

" This must be Merina's diary. And, oh! Here! Some pages had been ripped out! " Kevin said, so much excited. Genie looked at the book. Kevin was right.

" Hey! This handwriting! We - we had seen it before! " Genie said as a light flashed in her head.

" But I can't remember where. " Genie said, thinking hard.

" Oh! The note! " Kevin gasped. Genie looked at him.

" THE NOTE! THE NOTE! THAT NOTE ABOUT ANNE! " Kevin screamed. Genie, too gave a shriek. But her shriek continued and continued with great terror and Kevin clapped one of his hands over her mouth.

When Genie got back to her senses, Kevin took his hand off and the pair of them stood frozen, staring at each other.

" So, th - that was not a letter from Ant - tonella! It was - it was a part of M - Merina's diary. Merina is the one who killed Anne. Oh my! " Genie shuddered at the fact.

They both jumped when they heard someone clearing his throat loudly at the doorway and saw Minaz standing there. Kevin pushed the diary back into the bag rapidly and pulled out the homework book. Minaz walked towards them very slowly and it was a horrible scene.

Minaz stood right in front of the two children. Genie tried hard not to shiver, but she failed. Minaz gazed at them.

" Give it to me. " Minaz said. He held out his left hand. Kevin handed the homework book to him.

" Out! Now! " Minaz said and Genie and Kevin escaped from the classroom.

When they got down from the veranda, they broke into a run. Genie was the one who began to run, first. She did not know why she did it. But she ran as fast as she could. Kevin stood still for a moment then followed her, running.

They reached their favourite path and stopped there, panting. They gazed at each other.

" So? " Genie broke the silence. It was not right to say there was a complete silence, there were the voices of Genie and Kevin both panting.

" S - so? " Kevin repeated.

" Wh - what a - re - we - goi - ng - to - do? " Genie asked him.

" I - don't - know. " Kevin answered.

They stood in silence for minutes and caught their breath back.

" So, Antonella wasn't the one who killed Anne. It was Merina who killed the girl. But, how could it be true? " Genie was completely confused.

" I don't think Merina would ever dare to kill a girl. And Anne was her bestie, wasn't she? "

" Yes, she was. She had written ' my Anne ', remember? "

" Yeah, so... "

" So? "

" So... "

" So what? "

" It's too confusing, " said Kevin helplessly.

Genie and Kevin sat on their seats, silently and thoughtfully. Sintra was teaching, but they were hearing nothing. When the bell rang, Sintra left.

CHAPTER FIVE
ON THE STONE BENCH

Genie and Kevin looked at each other when they saw Merina coming towards them.

" Hello, " said Merina, smiling.

" H - hello, " said Genie and Kevin together. Merina looked over her shoulders. There was Antonella sitting on her table. Antonella nodded at her encouragingly. Merina turned back to Genie and Kevin. Merina closed her eyes for a moment and then took a deep breath and opened her eyes.

" I believe it's time, " said Merina.

" Er - sorry? "

" I believe it's time, " said Merina, " time to tell you every-thing. Please come with me. "

Merina walked straight out of the classroom and Genie and Kevin automatically followed her.

Merina led them to the playground. It was study time and the playground was empty. Merina sat on one of the stone benches beside the ground. Genie sat on her left side and Kevin sat beside Genie.

" You mean - you're going to tell us every secrets? " Genie

broke the silence.

" Yes. " Merina nodded.

" Abuot - about Anne and Rose and - and everything? " Genie heard herself asking and somehow she was sure Merina knew all those secrets. Merina nodded.

" Then, go on, Merina " Kevin said eagerly.

" First, I'm not Merina. " She said and Genie and Kevin gave a small laugh.

" You're kidding... "

" No, I'm not, " said Merina sharply and they both stopped laughing. "I'm not kidding, " said Merina, " I'm not Merina. I'm Maria. "

Genie and Kevin froze.

" I am Maria and the one who not comes to school since the trip to Littlegreen Zoo is Merina " said Maria.

" So? "

" So, " said Maria, " Merina is not going to another school and she is not staying in Grandma's house. She - Oh, I will tell the whole story. Let me start from the very beginning. " Maria sat more comfortably on the bench and Genie and Kevin waited eagerly for the words to fell out of Maria's mouth.

"OK, " said Maria, " my Mum and Dad are both Tiger-People. Their tigers are living happily in a jungle far away. We goes to visit the forest in holidays. And I and Merina are Tiger-Girls, too. But we both did not know where our tigers were. And Merina is friends with Leda, your sister " Maria added looking at Kevin, and she continued

"Leda shared her feelings and thoughts with her. Once she told Merina that she has strange feeling about tigers. So, Merina and I were sure that Leda was a Tiger-Girl. Merina loved her a lot and she decided to gave her a surprise. Merina decided to find Leda's tiger. She searched and searched.

We have so many relatives who are Tiger-People and she searched with the helps of them"

" Merina, sorry, Maria, how we can find someone's tiger without them? " It was Genie's doubt.

" We can find someone's tiger without them. First, we have to know their interests. Means - things like their favourite colour, favourite hobbies and like that. Then we have to find is there any tiger with the same interests"

"If there any tiger with the same interests as a Tiger-One, it is his or her tiger"

"There are special secret Centres by specialist Tiger-People. There, they has so many tigers. Their duty is to find those tigers' Tiger-People. Isn't it nice? And Merina visited many centres like that with Dad. At last, they found a tigress with the same interests as Leda. They brought that tigress to our house from its Centre.

We looked after the tigress. Merina thought first, she have to make Leda know all these things. Little Leda know nothing about Tiger-People. So, Merina have to explain. First, she gave Leda a small nice picture. A picture of a tiger. So, like she had expected, Leda's feel began to grow wilder. Merina tried all the ways to make it happen. And Leda's feel grew wilder and wilder day by day

Finally, Merina decided to explain everything to her. On the day before the day she had decided to explain, Anne came. Anne was Merina's bestest best friend. I has no role in their friendship. Anne was coming or our house for the first time since Leda's tigress came to our house.

Anne's parents were going out and Anne was coming to spend a night in our house. Merina was so glad. They played together for a long time and then everybody went to sleep. I woke up hearing a loud scream that morning. I ran down to the living room. There, Merina was screaming, horrified.

I asked her what happened. She pointed at the tigress. It was licking its lips. Anne was not there. Merina said when she woke and went to Anne's room to wake her, the room was empty. She searched everywhere. When she came to the living room, she saw the tigress standing there like that. So, Leda's tigress killed Anne and ate her"

" Excuse me, how can a tigress eat a human being without leaving any bone or hair? " Kevin asked Maria. It was the same doubt that was pounding inside Genie.

"A tiger or tigress can eat something without leaving bones or hair once. Only once in a lifetime" sighed Maria.

" well, " she continued

"Merina got very upset. She thought she was the reason of Ann's death. She was the one who decided it was the living room for the tigress to sleep. It was the morning of the Littlegreen Zoo trip, you know.

Merina laid in her bed crying and sobbing. I came to the trip. Then in the zoo, I realized you are a Tiger-Girl, Genie. When I got back to home, Merina was still crying. I told her Genie is a Tiger-Girl. But Merina was very sad and upset about Anne. She believed she is the one who led Anne to such a painful death and it seemed like she was growing mad. She wrote terrible things in her diary and I had to hide her diary in my school bag.

Mum and Dad thought if we would find Merina's tiger, it would be a great consoling to her. Dad and Mum found that Merina's tigress is in the Littlegreen Zoo.

They told Merina. Merina decided to play a dangerous game. She coloured her hair to red. Deep red... pure red... she did many strange make-ups and changed her appearance"

" Rose! " Genie gasped. She clapped her hands over her mouth.

" Yes, Rose, " said Maria, " Rose Ginch. Maria was Rose. She started to work. She kept visiting Arasenmosis. He is a leader to all the Tiger-People in the world. Mum and Dad told her about him. Merina and Arasenmosis became good friends. She told him all these secrets. He told her another secret. He told her about Fireglow. The secret underground place. It was made by some old Tiger-People, long long ago. He gave a magical key too"

"Merina decided to go through it and rescue her tigress Toma. Before that, she had to explain things to you. And she won in that mission. She and you rescued Toma and Tigo "

Maria finished and Genie and Kevin were sitting with their mouths hanging open.

" So, the one whom we saw near the trapdoor was you, right? " Genie asked, trying hard to recover from the shock.

" Yeah, " replied Maria,

" it was me. It all was a drama. A drama to attract you two to all these. Merina - as Rose - once asked you if you know Genie, hadn't she Kevin? And I was too upset and ,ad when we met near the trapdoor, wasn't I? We knew you two would be determined to take the risk and find things out. That was what we wanted. And now everything is success."

" What about Anne's parents? Didn't they question your parents? " Kevin asked eagerly.

" It's a mystery, " said Maria mistily, " Anne's parents never returned. Her house is still left locked. "

" Minaz knew all these? " Gene asked her.

" Yep, " answered Maria, " he is a close friend of Dad's and he tells everything to Mr Minaz. "

" Horrible. He is rude, isn't he? " Genie said truthfully.

" Who? Mr Minaz? " Maria asked, surprised.

" Yep, " said Kevin and Genie nodded.

" No! He just acts like he is. He is nice. He is kind, " said Maria. Genie loved to change the topic.

" Antonella knew? " Genie asked her.

" She found out accidently, " said Maria.

" What d'you mean? Accidently? " Genie and Kevin asked together.

" Yeah, " sighed Maria, " one day, she saw Merina's diary in my bag. "

" How? "

" I opened my bag to take my homework book, " said Maria nervously, " and then she saw the diary. You know, she has a bad habit of peeping on others' matters. Anyway, she pulled the diary out. I tried to grab it back. But she had already opened it. I grabbed it. She pulled it again and it totally got worse. The final result was that some pages were sitting in Antonella's hands, ripped out of the book. She ran away and read those. So, she knew a small part of the secrets and I had no choice but tell her the rest. And I did. Then she got scared of Tiger-People. That was why she was not talking to you, Genie. I tried to explain

Tiger-People are not dangerous. Then she gave the papers back and one fell down and you know what happened next.

Then I did not know Mr Minaz knew everything. That was why I told you to throw it out. And Mr Minaz told you to take my homework book, didn't he? He did it to make you find the diary. "

" Then why didn't you just come straight to us and tell us all these? " Kevin asked.

"Because, Merina was not in a good condition. She was not willing to explain all those straight to you. She was not willing to you to know that she was the reason of Anne getting killed straight. She was sure if you heard all the story straight, you would hate her. You would think she had killed Anne. And now, after all these adventures, you would never think bad about Merina" Maria finished simply.

" OK. I think thats enough, now you three must go to the classroom. " They heard a cold void from behind them and turned to find Minaz standing behind the stone bench with a thin smile.

CHAPTER SIX
ANNE LOZWARD

That day was a day of shock to Genie and Kevin. They could not concentrate in any of the lessons. Rose, Arasenmosis, Maria, Merina, Anne... all these names were pounding on their ears. Every now and then, they would throw sideway glances at Antonella and Maria.

When the final bell rang, all ran out of the classroom hurrily and cheerfully, all except Genie Razi, Kevin Notts, Maria Yumia and Antonella Foa. They took their bags and walked out of the classroom, slowly and silently.

" Come to my house. " Maria broke the silence.

" Wh -" Genie began, but then Elsa called from the left side cheerfully:

" Hey, Merina! "

" Hi, " Maria called back.

" Hey, hello Genie. And Kevin and Antonella. " Elsa was in a really happy mood.

" Hello, " said Genie, Kevin and Antonella gloomily.

When Elsa passed, Genie asked in a whisper:

" What? "

" You and Kevin come to my house, " Maria murmured back.

" For what? " Kevin muttered.

" Or meet my twin sister. " On this answer, Genie or Kevin said nothing but followed her to her own house. Antonella departed on the way.

Genie, Kevin and Maria walked together.

" Wow! " Genie said heartily. They were on a lovely place. A small blue stream was flowing near the green grasses and there were trees all around. Yellow flowers were peeping out of the grasses.

Maria smiled. Kevin knew how Genie would react in such an occasion. He had been her best friend ever since they began to study in that school and he knew how much interested Genie was in lovely places. She did exactly the same Kevin was expecting.

She dropped her bag swiftly on the grass and ran to the stream. She jumped from rock to rock through the stream and cried:

" WOO-HOO! HOW ENCHANTING! "

" We have no time to play. If you like this place, you can come and spend a holiday in my house. Now, we have to go, " said Maria. It took a long time for her and Kevin to make Genie leave that place.On the rest of the journey, Genie was singing and watching around happily and was smiling brightly to herself.

A big house came to sight. It was surrounded by trees and made Genie gave another hearty " wow... " Maria knocked at the green door. There was no answer. She knocked again and again and they heard footsteps hurrying down and Merina's voice called dully from inside:

" Coming... "

The door opened and Genie saw Rose standing at the

doorway.

" Oooooh! Rose? " Genie gasped.

" I told you, " reminded Maria.

" Oh, right, " said Genie, " hello, Maria - I mean Merina. "

" H - hello, " said Rose.

" Why didn't you take all those make-ups down? " Maria asked.

" Nothing, " said Rose, " come in. "

They sat in the living room. Genie had called her mum in the phone in the house and told her she was in Kevin's house. Kevin's lie to his mum was he was in Genie' s house.

" One minute, " saying so, Rose ran upstairs.

" She's going to take all those make-ups off. You can see 'Rose' coming back as 'Merina', " said Maria, smiling.

It was true, after some time, Merina came back downstairs.

" You told them everything? " Merina asked Maria. Maria nodded triumphantly.

" Now, it's a happy ending, " said Maria brightly. But, Merina sighed sadly and looked upstairs. A tigress came down.

" Leda's? " Genie asked.

" Yeah, " answered Maria.

Tears appeared in Merina's eyes.

" Zia, " said Maria and Genie and Kevin looked at her.

" The tigress? " Genie said.

" Yep. Her name is Zia, " said Maria.

" Come on, " Maria said quickly as she watched Merina preparing to cry, let's go out, it's a good weather. "

They got to their feet and walked out of the house.

Maria was abselutely right about the weather. It was the rainy seaoson, but the sun was shining brightly but softly. They sat by a blue pond surrounded by grasses.

Then Zia, the tigress came there.

" Go away, " Merina said angrily, " for what you came? To kill and eat one of us? Yeah, right, then go ahead! Kill me, eat me! " Merina's voice was furious and mad.

" Hey, " said Genie who felt sympathetic about the poor tigress, "leave it, Merina. " Genie patted Merina on the back.

Zia sat silently on the grass. Genie felt sad. Then they heard a noise. It was from a green bush and then a little rabbit jumped out. Another hearty " wow " fell from Genie's mouth. The rabbit was small and furry and was very white. It had red eyes.

The poor bunny stopped dead at sight of the tigress. Zia jumped towards the bunny and Genie gasped. The bunny tried to run away, but Zia caught it with her strong paws. The bunny squeaked. Zia bit the bunny on the neck. Genie clapped her hands over her mouth and jumped to her feet.

" No, " said Genie and she ran towards the furious tigress. Genie was determined to save the rabbit. She bent down and tried to make Zia release the poor struggling bunny.

" GENIE! NO! " Kevin screamed and came running with Maria and Merina. Zia growled and hit Genie hard on the stomach with the head. Genie fell backwards and hit the grassy ground.

" Ah, " she gave a small shriek.

" Genie, " Kevin helped her back to her feet.

The squeak of the bunny grew fainter and fainter. Genie was struggling to save it, but Kevin's tight arms were not releasing her. She watched the tigress killing the bunny with tearful eyes.

Zia killed the bunny. Its struggles ended and it laid motionless. Zia looked at it cruelly and began to eat it. Zia ate the bunny rapidly. She ate it without leaving any bone or fur or anything. Even little drops of blood.

Genie burst into tears. Kevin knew she would. He knew

how she loved animals. He knew how soft is her heart towards animals.

" Come on, it's just a rabbit. Leave it. Come on, " said Kevin consolingly and they all got into the house.

When they all sat in the living room, Genie remembered something.

" Hey! " Genie said, very much shocked.

" What? " The others asked her, nervously.

" Maria, you said a tiger or tigress can eat something without leaving any bone or hair or things like that only once in a lifetime, didn't you? " Genie asked in a shocked voice. Maria nodded, puzzled.

" So, Zia can eat something in that way only once, right? And -"

" And she ate Anne in that way, " said Merina, leaving Genie in midsentence.

" Wait, " Genie said slolwy, " wait, Merina, wait. Zia ate the bunny in that way now. She can eat something in that way only once. And she ate the bunny in that way in front of us. So, how can we say she had eaten Anne in that way? "

Kevin, Merina and Maria jumped at the idea.

" SO? " Merina squealed.

" So, Zia had not eaten Anne, " said Genie.

" Oh, Genie, " said Merina and she ran towards Genie and hugged her so tightly that she fell down backwards.

" Then what happened to Anne? " Kevin asked as Genie sat straight again.

" That's the question, " said Genie seriously, " that's the question -"

" And here is the answer of that question. " Genie, Kevin, Maria and Merina all jumped when they heard a strong voice from behind.

They turned and saw a tall man at the doorway. He had

a well-shaved face and black hair. His dark eyes were sparkling with tears.

" Mr Lozward? " Merina gasped.

" Yes, Roaz Lozward, " said the man. Maria and Merina both clapped their hands over their mouths.

" Who are you? " Genie heard herself asking.

" I told you, " said Mr Loaward, " Roaz Lozward. "

" Who is Mr Lozward? " Genie asked Maria and Merina, slowly.

" He - he is - father of - father - of -" Merina's voice was shaking.

" Of? " Genie said, her eyes narrowed.

" Father of Anne, " Maria finished the sentence and Genie clapped her hand over her mouths, too.

" You're - you're back? " Genie said in a shaky voice.

" Yes, I am, " said Mr Lozward.

" Father of Anne? " Kevin spoke for the first time after Mr Loaward arrived.

" Yes, father of Anne Lozward, " said Mr Lozward.

" When? When you came back? " Maria asked him.

" Just now, " he answered.

" Is Mrs Lozward with you? " Maria asked again.

" Yes, " Mr Lozward nodded, " she is in the house. "

" What happened to Anne? " it was Merina who asked this time and she was completely tearful.

" Anne is not dead. She is alive. But -" his voice began to shake more sadly, " but she's gone!"

" What d'you mean? She is alive. But she is gone? " Merina asked him, more tearfully.

" Mr Lozward, please sit down and tell us the whole story, " said Maria and they all settled down on the sofa.

" My wife and I - we're not Tiger-People. We're ordinary people. Merina, you told Anne all about Tiger-People and all and she told us. And, once, my wife and I had to go to visit a long cousin. Her name's Jasmine. Jasmine Ewergia. She's an old woman. She's a cousin of the sister of the mother of the wife of the younger brother of my mother's. We had to go and see her because she was ill and was in her deathbed. Anne was not interested in meeting someone whom she hadn't seen in her life before. She didn't want to come. I told you, it was a long cousin of mine and Anne, even my wife hadn't seen her before. So, Anne came here. my wife and I were in the cousin Jasmin's house. Days passed. Now morning, we got a letter, See" Mr Lozward took a small letter out of his pocket.

He handed it to the children. It was a piece of a faded, yellowing paper. The letter was in a shaky handwriting and it was clear that the hand of the one who wrote it was trembling.

Genie, Kevin, Maria and Merina began to read.

' Dear Mum and Dad,

I found I am a Tiger-Girl. I has all the feelings that Merina told me a Tiger-Girl would have. And I'm going to find my tiger. I promise you I would come back, after I found my tiger. Bye.

- Your Anne. '

Genie handed the letter back to Mr Lozward with trembling hands.

" My wife and I got mad when we read this and we searched for her. For all these days, we were in search for her, but we couldn't find our daughter. Now we came back to see if there's any sign of her, here. " Mr Lozward sighed sadly.

" There's nothing here... " said Merina, tears running down her cheeks.

There was a pause. Genie was staring at the window with

watery eyes. Kevin was gazing blankly at the floor. Maria was watching her twin sister. Merina was weeping silently. There were no sobs or sniffing from her. Only tears rolling down her pale cheeks. Mr Lozward was trying hard to not let the tears that were sparkling in his eyes come out.

" I would better go, " it was Mr Lozward who broke the silence. The children looked at him. He got to his feet.

" Bye kids, " he walked to the doorway and disappeared from view. No one spoke or moved.

After a frozen silence, Merina let out a sigh and wiped her tears away. When she wiped one teardrop away, another one came running down. When she got her fingers there to wipe it away, another three fell from the other eye. After a long time's rubbing on the face, the tears vanished from her face, but her face was too red because of the rubbing.

Merina looked at Genie. Genie saw a little bit of hope in those eyes. Genie felt she had to do something.

Genic stood up. Kevin, Maria and Merina looked at her.

" I think " said Genie in a strong voice" the new adventures begin here. We have to find her. We have to find Anne. We must do it. And... we will do it. "

There was a pause. Then Merina stood up.

" I will be with you. " Her voice was suddenly strong.

" I will be with you, " said Kevin and Maria together, getting to their feet.

CHAPTER SEVEN
INTO THE
GREEN HEART

Genie got to her house, determined. It was getting dark when she returned.

Rachel was sitting in the veranda, as Genie had expected. Rachel smiled and got to her feet.

" Why are you so late? You were playing in Kevin's house, I know, I know," said Rachel with a naughty smile. Genie said nothing but got into the house. Rachel followed her. Genie met her dad, David in the living room.

" Hello Genie, " he said.

" Dad, Mum, I've got a very important thing to tell you, " said Genie, seriously. She told the whole story to her parents.

When she finished, Rachel and David sat with their eyes widened, mouths hanging open.

" And are you going to find her? What's her name - ah, Anne. And are you going to find Anne? " David asked her. Genie nodded.

" Genie, you had read countless magical books. And now you're telling us one wonderful fantasy story -" Rachel began, but then Genie said a little hotly:

" It is not a fantasy story, Mum. It's a fantasy in real life. "

" Oh, Genie, you have a wonderful ability of telling a fantasy story, making it look like a real one. Why don't you write all this as a book? " Rachel said brightly.

" Oh, Mum! It's not a fantasy story. It's real. How can I explain you, " Genie said, completely puzzled about how she was going to make her parents believe her.

" Ah, wait. I will be back in no time, " Genie said, getting to her feet.

" Where are you going? " Rachel and David stood up.

" I will be back in no time, " Genie repeated and she was already at the doorway.

" Now? It's night, " Rachel reminded, her eyes narrowing.

Genie got out of the room so quickly, ignoring her parents.

" Mum, Dad, who can come with me? " Genie asked them. Rachel and David looked at each other.

" I will, " David hurried down.

" Me too, " Rachel came, too.

" The car... " Genie said.

They all got to the car. David sat in the driving seat. Genie sat in the seat beside him. Rachel sat on the back seat. Genie gave instructions to her father about where to go. Finally, the car stopped in front of the house of the Yumia family.

" Where are we now? " Rachel asked, looking out of the window.

" This is Maria and Merina's house, " answered Genie seriously.

" Mum and Dad stay in the car. I will be back soon, " Genie said. She pushed the door open and stepped out of the car. She turned and slammed the door.

Genie crossed the grassy ground and knocked at the

Yumia house door. A thin, black-haired woman opened the door.

" Er - Mrs Yumia? " Genie said in a low voice.

" Yes, " said the woman, a little surprised to see a little girl at the doorway at night.

" I'm Genie, " replied Genie.

" Oh, " said Mr Yumia as though she had just got a flash of memory in her head.

"Genie Razi? "

" Yeah, "

" Come in, come in. "

Genie got into the house with Mrs Yumia.

" Maria!, Merina! Come! " Mrs Yumia called, looking up at the staircase. Maria and Merina came down the stairs and greeted Genie warmly. It was easy for her to explain because Maria, Merina and Mrs Yumia knew the whole story.

" So," said Genie.

" I have to prove that the story I told my parents is right. If I did so, they would help us. "

" OK, " said Maria,

" You can. I've brought Tigo and Toma here. You know-not-me I mean Merina's Rose"

" Tigo! Tigo! " Genie called. After some seconds, the tiger came downstairs.

" Bye, " Genie waved in farewell and walked out of the house with Tigo.

When they got near the car, Rachel gasped at sight of the tiger. Tigo began to roar, but Genie said:

" Tigo, it's my Mum and Dad, " and he stopped roaring.

Genie pulled the back door open and Tigo jumped in. Rachel let out a scream and jumped.

" Mum, it's Tigo. My pet, " said Genie, getting into the car and slamming the door close.

The car moved. Rachel was staring fixedly at Genie. Tigo curled up on Genie's feet.

" Now, you see... it's the truth, " said Genie. Rachel or David said nothing.

" I was not telling a magical fantasy story. It's the truth, " said Genie again. Slowly, Rachel nodded, still looking shocked.

The moonlight was flowing all over the road and trees beside. There were only a few vehicles on the road. The wind was so cold but soft. There was the warmth of the tiger's fur on Genie's feet.

It was a silent journey. When the car stopped in the yard of the house of the Razi family, Genie was the one who got out first. After her, Tigo jumped out. And then came Mr and

Mrs Razi slowly.

They entered the house. The lights turned on.

" I'd make the supper" said Rachel quickly and went to the kitchen as though escaping from the frozen silence. David looked at Genie. She said nothing. Tigo walked around them.

" I've got some works to do " David, too escaped from the frozen silence into his books and papers.

Genie was the only one left. But it was not an uncomfortable frozen silence to her. She smiled at Tigo and sat beside him. She sat, resting her head on the warm fur of the tiger and smiling to herself in a very pretty way.

Minutes passed. Genie did not know how long she sat like that. But then, the voice of Rachel called :

" Supper is ready, come and eat. " Genie got to her feet and went to the dining room.

There, David was already at the dining table. Genie and

Rachel settled down in two chairs.

" Er - what to give the tiger to eat? " Rachel asked shyly. Genie looked at her.

" He'd like meat, " said Genie. She stood up and went to her room. Jane and Sam was there. Genie took Sam's plate and came back to the dining room. She put a lot of meat in the plate and placed it in front of the tiger. He began to eat. Then Genie started to eat.

Genie came to the living room and began to watch a Spanish movie in the television. Tigo sat on the sofa with her. David and Rachel joined them, halfway through the movie.

When the movie ended, Rachel got to her feet and said:

" Genie dear, it's time to sleep. "

Genie stood up.

" Goodnight, " said David.

" Goodnight, Dad, " said Genie. She walked silently into her room. Rachel and Tigo followed her.

When Genie was climbing onto her bed, Rachel asked shyly again :

" Er - what about the tiger? "

" Oh, Tigo... no problem... leave him here... he will stay with me... "

Genie said smilingly.

Rachel thought for a moment and then nodded. She bent down and kissed her daughter on the forehead. Genie kissed her mother on the cheek.

" Goodnight, Genie. "

" Goodnight, Mum. "

Rachel left the room, closing the door behind her. Genie climbed out of the bed and turned the light on. Jane and Sam were sitting in a corner shyly. Genie knew why.

" Oh, dears... you two are as much important to me as

Tigo is..." she said kindly and walked towards them.

Genie bent down and took Sam in her arms. He was her favourite. She ran her fingers through his warm fur. Sam closed his little eyes. Jane growled. Genie gave a small laugh.

"Oh, Jane! You little jealous girl!" Genie put Sam down and took Jane. Now, Jane looked happier and satisfied.

Genie put the cat in bed. Then the pup climbed onto the bed, determined.

"Come on," Genie whispered to the tiger. Tigo jumped onto the bed and Sam and Jane moved into the very corner of the bed.

"Oh, you foolish kids... Tigo is your friend. Why are you being so shy and scared of him?" Genie said and she took Sam in her arms.

Sam tried to move away, but Genie placed him on the back of the tiger. Sam sat there, looking round at Genie, as though pleading for help.

"Sit there," said Genie, smiling brightly. Sam sat on the back of Tigo. After a while, the pup looked like he had started to enjoy it. Tigo, too seemed enjoying it. Jane growled jealously and jumped onto the back of Tigo. They all began to play.

Jane pushed Sam out and sat on his place like a queen. Poor Sam was hanging on the left ear of Tigo.

"Ooohh..." Genie helped him to climb back. He faced Jane like a returned king. Sam pushed her and she fell onto the bed. Genie took Sam and put him near Jane. Jane looked at Genie thankfully. Seeing the expression on Sam's face, Genie laughed out.

Sam jumped onto her head and started to pull her hair with his sharp nails.

"Ha! Oh, Tigo... help me... ha ha ha!" Genie was screaming and was laughing at the same time. Tigo took her words in heartily and jumped forward and pushed Sam down. Genie laughed.

Genie took a pillow and threw it at the tiger. The tiger growled and jump to her. She was pinned to the soft bed by his naughty paws. Genie tried to release herself, laughing, but she failed. Tigo was too strong.

Fortunately, Genie's left hand reached a pillow. She took the pillow and hit the tiger softly on the face with it. Tigo turned his face away and tried to scratch it with his paws. Then, Genie was released. She laughed again.

This sort of things continued for a long time. Genie threw one of the pillows at Sam. But Tigo jumped and caught it. Then Jane ran and hit the pillow. Genie laughed heartily. The pillow went flying and landed on the floor with a thud. Genie jumped down the bed, still laughing. She bent down. She took the pillow and straightened herself up, still laughing. She froze. Her laugh fainted and her smile faded away. The door was open and her mother Rachel was standing at the doorway, watching her.

" Er - Mum, erm... " Genie said slowly. Rachel looked so serious. " Er - erm... oh! " Genie grinned. Rachel did not. Genie grinned from ear to ear. Slowly, a very small smile began to play on Rachel's lips. She tried to press it off, but she could not.

" Anyway, " said Rachel.

" Anyway? Will you join us in our pillow fight, Mum? Oh, it would be wonderful! " Genie cried overjoyed.

" What? Get to you bed and sleep, naughty girl! Quick! Quick! " Rachel said in a high pitched voice.

Genie made a disappointed expression and climbed onto her bed. She layed beside Tigo.

" Goodnight, Mum, " said Genie, closing her eyes.

" Oi! Girl! are you going to sleep with a pup, a cat and a tiger? " Rachel demanded.

" Yeah, " said Genie and she felt nothing extraordinary with it.

" Ho! What a child you are! Sam, come down! Come, come! And you, Jane! Er - get that tiger down, " said Rachel. Sam and Jane curled up on the floor, disappointed. Tigo jumped down and layed on the floor with them.

" It's already midnight. No playing! Sleep. Goodnight, " said Rachel and she turned the light off and left.

Genie sprang out of the bed, the moment her mother's footsteps went away. Sam and Jane looked at her, hopefully.

" I know it's too cold on the floor, dears. I know the floor is cold as ice. Come, " said Genie. At the moment she spoke these words, the pup, cat and the tiger jumped up onto the bed.

Genie got to bed, too. She layed beside Tigo. She put one of her arms around him and closed her eyes, whispering

" goodnight... "

On the next morning, the soft sunlight streamed into the room through the windowsills. The sunlight knocked softly at Genie's eyelids and she opened them. She laid still for two minutes or so with her eyes open to drive the sleepiness away. When she felt she had driven her sleepiness away, she got out of bed.

After brushing her teeth and taking a bath, she came out of the bathroom. Tigo and Sam were sitting in the bed. Jane the laziest cat Genie had ever seen was still sleeping.

Genie came to them.

" Genie? " Genie heard her mother calling from outside the room.

" Yes, Mum. " She replied.

" Ah, the breakfast is ready, " said Rachel's voice.

" I'm coming, Mum, " said Genie, bending down over Jane.

" Jane, " she whispered, " Jane, wake up! "

The lazy cat opened her eyes, slowly.

" Mum's calling, " said Genie, " get out of bed, girl. You know, Mum won't like you sleeping in my bed... "

Jane closed her eyes lazily again, as though she had heard nothing from Genie.

" Oh, you lazy girl... " Genie took Jane in her hands. She placed the cat on a cushion that was laying on the floor for her. Jane laid there.

Sam and Tigo were already on the floor. Genie ran to the door and opened it.

" Good morning, Mum, " said Genie brightly.

" Good morning, " said Rachel, " come, have some break-fast... "

Rachel entered the room and she went straight to Sam and Jane. Genie watched her mother bending down and taking Sam in her hands. Rachel tried to wake Jane. But Jane ignored her and continued to sleep.

" Oh, you lazy creature, come on... " Rachel said and she dropped Sam down and started to shake Jane. Jane half opened her eyes and then closed them again. Rachel shook her again and again.

" Oh, you cat, I'm getting angry... come on... " Rachel's voice grew angrier and her shaking grew harder.

" Hey, you lazy creature! Come! Come! " As Rachel's words grew into shouts, Genie said, walking towards her :

" Wait, Mum. "

Genie got to her knees and touched Jane slowly.

" Jane... come on dear... wake up... there's a delicious breakfast waiting for you... come on... " Genie murmured softly.

Slowly, Jane opened her eyes.

" Ah! Good girl! " Genie said cheerfully, taking the cat up.

" See, this is the way to talk to pets, " Genie said proudly to her mother, running her fingers through the ginger fur of Jane, who was now laying in her hands.

" OK, Sam, come on, " said Rachel and Sam ran to her and started to lick her feet.

" And... " the same shyness came to Rachel's words, " the tiger... "

" Tigo, come, " Genie said casually. Tigo came towards her and Rachel moved two steps away.

They all got to the dining hall. David was at the table, eating fast and well-dressed to go to work.

" Good morning, Dad. " Genie said, sitting down.

" Good morning, " said David.

Rachel was busy with feeding the animals. David finished his food and departed when Genie was halfway through her food. After three minutes or so, David came out from his study room with his bag.

" Bye, Genie " he said hurriedly.

" Bye, " Genie said through a piece of bread.

" I'm going, Rachel, " he said to his wife.

" Oh, yeah, bye, " said Rachel.

After finishing her food, Genie went to her own room. Tigo, Sam and Jane followed her. Genie closed the door and started to change. She took her pink frock of and put on her school uniform, bright blue shirt and black skirt. Then Genie stop in front of the clear mirror and started to comb her hair. She put a blue hair band on her hair.

Then she came to her study table. She pushed her notebooks, textbooks, pencils, pens and all into her school bag.

After getting her bag ready, Genie opened the door and got out.

Tigo, Sam and Jane followed her again. Genie got to the veranda. She sat on the single chair there and put on her shoes and socks. Rachel came there.

" Bye, Mum, " Genie said.

" Bye, " said Rachel.

" Bye, Sam... and Jane... and Tigo... " Genie jumped down with her bag shaking on her shoulders.

Genie waved at her mother, the tiger, the pup and the cat. Rachel waved back and went back into the house to get ready to go to her coffee shop.

Genie walked, humming one of her favourite songs. She walked for ten or twelve minutes and reached the classroom.

Like everyday, Kevin came and greeted her and she greeted him back. Genie started to play with Kevin, Georgina and Niaf. Their game ended when Sintra entered.

* * *

After school, Genie and Kevin were walking out of the classroom and then Maria and Antonella came hurrying to them.

" Genie, Kevin, we have an important thing to tell you, " said Maria.

" What is it? " Genie asked her.

" Come, " Maria jumped down the varandah. Genie, Kevin and Maria followed her.

As they walked, Maria said seriously :

" We should go. "

" What you mean? " Genie asked.

" We should go, " repeated Maria.

" What? I mean - where? " Kevin asked.

" To find Anne, " said Antonella and Genie and Kevin froze.

" Now? " Kevin broke the silence which was short-lived but looked like it would be long lived.

" Yes, " said Maria.

" But -" Genie began, hoping Maria or Antonella would say something and leave her in misdsentence, but they didn't. So, she herself stopped in the " but "

" So, first, Genie and Kevin, you two write a note each to your houses. And then we should leave. Antonella had already written the note. She had given that note to Elsa. She will give to Antonella's parents. " Maria said simply.

" We are going to go - straight? " Kevin asked slowly, his eyes narrowed than ever.

" Mr Minaz will come with us, " said Maria and Genie and Kevin's mouths fell open.

" Minaz? " Genie uttered the word with great disgust and her eyes were narrowing, too.

" Yes, " said Antonella, " he will come with us and he will help us. He is very brave. If he is with us, no danger can touch us. "

" I am not coming if that Minaz donkey is coming with us... " said Genie.

" Don't be so childish, Genie, " said Maria sharply.

" But, but -" this time, Genie had something to say after the " but ", but Maria said :

" Genie, I thought you were a brave girl and now I'm disappointed to find you are not. "

Genie felt a lightning running through her insides.

" I promise you, you would never be disappointed in the matter of my courage! " Genie said in a strong voice, her head held high.

" Good! And what about you, Kevin? " Maria turned to Kevin.

" Er -" Kevin began, but then Antonella said:

" No 'er', Kevin. "

" Fine, " said Kevin, " if Genie's coming... I will come. "

" Good! " Antonella said proudly, with a sideway glance at Maria.

" But, Maria, we are going to find Anne, right? And we don't have any clue about where is she. Then, where we are going to go? " Genie asked Maria.

" We h -" Maria began, but Antonella broke in :

" We have a clue. "

" What? " Genie and Kevin both jumped.

" Anne is somewhere in the South Forests. " Antonella said and she looked at Maria triumphantly and Maria turned her face away from her.

" H - how you got the c - clue? " Genie asked.

" Mr Jola. " Antonella said.

" Oh, Antonella, would you please stop telling head and tail and tell them something clearly? " Maria said, her eyebrows raised up.

" Fine. " Antonella said furiously.

" Mr Jola told Mr Minaz, today morning. Mr Jola said his brother is living near the South Forests. He had seen a little girl there. So, Anne went there hoping her tiger would be there. " Maria explained.

" So, we're going to the South Forests? " Genie said, very thrilled.

" Yes, " said Maria.

Genie, Kevin, Maria and Antonella came back to their classroom. The classroom was empty. There was no one but them. The four of them sat down on the floor in a circle. Genie took her bag off her shoulders and placed it in front of her. Kevin did the same.

Genie and Kevin opened their bags and took out papers, notebook and pen. Genie put the notebook in her lap and placed a clean white paper on it. She began to scribble.

' Dear Mum and Dad,

I'm going. Don't get worried, I'll come back safely. I told you about Anne, remember... and now, we got a clue about where's she. So, we're going... please don't tell anyone about this. If you think there's any problem, or if we don't return in time, you can tell Mr and Mrs Yumia or Mr and Mrs Notts or Mr and

Mrs Foa or Mr Jola, OK? Bye... love you...

- Your Genie. '

Genie finished her note and passed it to Maria and Antonella to read. Just then, Kevin finished scribbling his own note.

" Show me, " said Genie. Kevin handed the paper to her. She started to read.

' Dear Mum and Dad,

I've got a lot of things to tell you. But there's no time enough to explain, now. So, let me tell you the most important fact, I'm going. When you got this note, don't get panicked and run to report the Police. Just contact Mr or Mrs Yumia. They'll explain. See you soon...

- With a lot of love,

Your Kevin. '

" This's OK, Genie, " said Antonella, handing the note back to Genie.

" Let me read, " Kevin took the note from Genie's hands.

" Now, read this, " said Genie, giving Kevin's note to Maria and Antonella. Kevin read Genie's note and gave it back to her and Maria and Antonella read Kevin's note and gave it back to him.

" How we're going to send these notes to our parents? " Genie asked Maria and Antonella.

" Looza will do it, " said Antonella, simply. Lora Looza was the caretaker of the school. A kind young woman.

" Yes, "nodded Maria, " Mr Minaz told her he had to pass some important note to his students' parents. "

Somebody entered the classroom. It was Minaz.

" Finished? " He asked in his usual dirty way. Genie ignored him.

" Yes, sir, " said Maria.

" Here, " said Antonella, taking her own note from her pocket and passing it to Minaz.

" And these, to the Razis and Nottses, " said Maria, taking Genie and Kevin's notes and handing them to Minaz.

Minaz took them and went out. They heard him talking to someone :

" Here's the notes from me to the house of Miss Razi, Miss Foa and Mr Notts. "

" Oh, I see, " said Miss Looza's voice.

" Er - sir, you're not giving complaints about the children, are you? " Miss Looza's voice said.

" That's none of your business, Looza. " Minaz's voice said sharply and Genie's anger towards him doubled.

" This is to the parents of the Razi, " said the voice of Minaz, and there was a rustling of a paper, " and this - to the parents of Foa, " a rustling sound of paper came again, " this to the Nottses"

" So, you can go, " said Minaz's voice.

" Oh, yeah, sir, " said Looza's voice and they heard her footsteps hurrying away.

Minaz came back to the classroom.

" So... let's go, " he said, his hands rubbing together. Genie, Kevin, Maria and Antonella got their feet.

" Ready? " Minaz asked.

" Yes, " it was Genie who said first. Then Kevin, Maria and Antonella repeated it.

" Good, " said Minaz, not looking at Genie.

" Come on, " he walked out of the classroom and the children followed him.

There was a super red car, parked on the far end of the yard of the classroom.

" Wow, " said Genie.

" Superb! " she said with her eyes fixed on the car.

" It's the latest model, " said Kevin, excited like her.

" Wonderful! I can't stop myself from jumping at the fact that we are going in that car! " Antonella cried.

" Nice, " said Maria.

Minaz gave a thin smile and got into the car. He sat in the driving seat.

" I will sit in the front seat, " said Maria enthusiastically.

" The fan of Minaz would sit beside him... I'm relieved I don't have to... " Kevin whispered in Genie's ear and she gave a small laugh.

" No, Maria, I'm sitting in the front seat, " said Antonella.

" No, " Maria said hurrily and she pulled the door open and got into the car and settled down in the front seat.

" Antonella, don't mind, let's sit together and enjoy the journey, " said Genie and a smile appeared in Antonella's disappointed face.

" I want the window seat, " said Genie.

" Window-seat-girl, " Kevin called her. He knew about Genie's great love towards window seats.

Antonella got to the back seat, first. Then Kevin followed her. Genie came next. She slammed the door shut. The car started. It ran out of the compound of the school. The car ran through the main road.

Genie sat, enjoying the cold wind whipping her hair. Nobody talked. The car stopped in front of the Yumia house. Mr and Mrs Yumia and Merina were waiting for them, outside the house.

" Bye, " said Merina and she kissed her parents. She had a very large backpack which was so full.

Merina came to the car. She sat beside Antonella. Maria poked her head out through the window and called :

" Bye, Dad! And bye, Mum! "

" Bye... " said Mr and Mrs Yumia, waving with a sad smile.

The car came back to the main road and began to travel southwards. Slowly, the bright blue of the sky began to darken. It grew darker and darker and silver stars appeared here and there. The night came. The sky was a deep, dark, inky blue and was starry and frozen. The wind was growing colder.

Then the stars began to hide themselves in the dark blankets of the black clouds. Of course, it started to rain.

The rain grew heavier and heavier and thunder and lightning came. The wind was stronger than ever. Surely, they were going to have a very rainy, cold night.

" I've got dresses for you all, " said Merina, opening her large bag.

" Oh, that's nice, " said Genie.

" This's for you, " said Merina, pulling a big plastic cover out of her bag and giving it to Genie. Genie looked into I. It was filled with dresses. Genie took out a black jacket and a scarf and put the rest of the dresses in her bag. She wore the warm jacket. She wrapped the scarf around her neck.

" Now, it feels a little warm and so much comfortable... " she said, satisfied. The others, too put on their jackets and scarves.

" Ahh... " said Genie. She always loved sitting in warm

dresses in cold, rainy weather.

" Could you please push that glass up? " Minaz said from the driving seat. Genie looked at Kevin.

" Could you, Razi? " Minaz said again. It was only then Genie noticed the all other windows of the car had been closed, but the window on her own side was still wide open.

" Oh, " Genie pushed the glass up, hurrily.

" What a disgusting girl... " Minaz said under his breath.

" I am not a disgusting girl, " said Genie hotly.

" Shut up, you disgusting Razi girl! " Minaz said loudly.

" I told you, I am not a disgusting girl, " said Genie sharply.

" I said SHUT UP! " Minaz shouted and Genie gave a gasp, but she opened her mouth to say some more, just then Kevin pinched on her hand and she looked at him and he told her to be silent.

There was a silence in the car. Nobody spoke. Genie was burning with the hot desire to shout at Minaz, but Kevin was not letting her to. For the first time in the journey, Genie felt trapped. She gave a sigh and rested her head on Kevin's shoulder.

The rain was pounding on the window glass... the car was rumbling... the road was laying long... the sky was dark... her eyelids were being heavy... the pounding... the rumbling... the length... the darkness... the heaviness... pound, pound... rumble, rumble... long, long... dark, dark... heavy, heavy... hmm... hmmmm...

Genie woke up. She did not know how long she slept. Her head was still resting on Keivn's shoulder and her eyelids were still heavy. But like she always does, she refused to sleep again. She hoped she would not accidently fall asleep again.

She took her head up from Kevin's shoulder and looked

at him. He was deep asleep. First, she began to wake him, but for some reason, she did not. Poor boy... sleep...

She looked at Antonella and Merina. Antonella was sleeping, too. Merina was sleeping with her head in Antonella's lap. Antonella, too was deep asleep. In the front seat, Maria was asleep, too. The only persons awake in the car were Genie and Minaz. She sighed.

Genie turned back to the window. It was not raining. Genie pushed the glass down and the cold wind rushed in. The wind was too cold and Genie gave a shudder. Her scarf was loosened and she tightened it quickly.

" Satisfied, Razi? " Minaz asked and Genie looked at him. She could only see the back of his head.

" Push the glass down, Razi, " said Minaz.

" Why should I? It's not raining! " Genie said a high pitched voice.

" I said push the glass down, Razi, " said Minaz again. Genie burst out.

" WHY ARE YOU COMMANDING ME? " Genie shouted and she lowered her voice a little at the thought of her sleeping friends,

" Why are you commanding me? You -"

" Fine, fine, you little girl. Stop shouting. Let my ears get some rest, " said Minaz, hotly.

Genie sat with her eyes fixed on the outside world. It was still dark outside. They were not in a city and it was clear that they were in a forested area.

Genie heard some movements beside her and she turned. Kevin was awake.

" Oh, you woke, " said Genie. But, Kevin said nothing and closed his eyes and fell asleep again.

" Oh, " Genie looked at him.

" How much he likes to sleep... " Genie whispered to herself. She rested her head on his shoulder.

The wind was howling... the car was rumbling... the road was laying long... the sky was dark... her eyelids were heavy... the howling... the rumbling... the length... the darkness... the heaviness... howl, howl... long, long... dark, dark... heavy, heavy...

hmm... hmmmm...

Genie woke up. All others except Minaz were sleeping. Genie looked out. The sky was still a deep, dark, inky blue. She sat like that for a long time. There were tired pale stars here and there. The stars looked so tired because of their sleepless waiting for the morning flower to bloom. Slowly, the stars disappeared like dim lights turning off, one by one.

On the far edge, where the sky hugs the dark treetops, the darkness of the blue of the sky began to fade. It turned into a light blue. Only there, the sky became a soft, clear, light blue.

Then, there came red. Some red lines appeared in that light blue corner of the sky. As Genie watched, the red started to grow. The red lines grew thicker and it became blood red. Within seconds, the red started fading. The red melted in the blue. And that corner of the sky was being filled with light blue, over and over, like a balloon being filled with air.

Comparing to the wide sky, that corner was a very little place. Finally, it burst. It burst with no sound, no harm, but with light blue spreading all over the sky. The morning came.

Genie felt satisfied that she watched the day dawning. She turned to Kevin. Then she suddenly felt disappointed that she had forgotten to wake him to watch the day dawning with her.

" Kevin, Kevin, " she shook him. Wrinkles appeared on his forehead.

" Let me sleep, Genie... " he whispered with disturbance and turned his face away, ready to fall asleep again.

" No, Kevin, see, it's morning. I waited till now. I hadn't wake you to watch the day dawning with me, had I? I waited and waited and now it's morning. And now, I have no choice but to wake you. Wake up, wake up, " said Genie.

" Oh, please, Genie... " murmured Kevin, holding his eyes shut more tightly.

Genie thought for a way to wake him. Then she got an idea. Genie cleared her thought and sang in a very childish voice she could ever make :

" Are you sleeping?

Are you sleeping?

Brother John - Oh, sorry - brother Kevin?

Brother Kevin?

Morning bells are -"

" Oh, Genie, fine... I'm awake... " said Kevin in tired voice, rubbing his eyes.

"Aha! Good boy! " Genie said cheerfully.

Kevin blinked and straightened up. He yawned and stretched his arms.

CHAPTER EIGHT
THE DARKNESS

Yes, Darwin Jola was on the tree.

" HEY, YOU DEVIL! " Minaz shouted and Jola looked down and stopped dead to see them.

" HOW CAN YOU ESCAPE? HA! " Minaz shouted at Jola who was blinking foolishly. Jola started to climb down, swiftly.

" AHA! COME ON! COME DOWN! " Genie yelled. Jola stopped, afraid.

" IF YOU'RE NOT GOING TO COME DOWN, " shouted Minaz,

" WE WILL COME THERE AND CATCH YOU! "

Slowly and fearfully, Jola came down. He tried to run away, the moment his feet touched the ground, but Minaz caught him. Jola tried to releas himself, but Minaz was too strong. Jola was struggling.

" Stay still, you monkey! " Minaz said angrily. Without a warning, Jola bent and gave a sharp bite on the left hand of Minaz.

" Ah! " Minaz screamed and took his hands off. Jola ran. But right then, Genie sped towards him and kicked him hard on the back. She was kicking him with the all strength she had and he fell down. Kevin and Minaz ran towards Genie and Jola. They caught him again.

Kevin looked around and saw a hard stone laying nearby. He took the large stone and hit Jola hard on the head with the stone. Jola let out a scream and then fainted with a bleeding head. Genie couldn't stop herself from gasping.

Genie, Kevin and Minaz dragged Jola to a tree and laid him there.

" Wait a minute, " said Minaz, " you, come with me. " Kevin and Minaz walked away. Suddenly they stopped and turned.

" Oh, you can't stay here alone... " Minaz said to Genie.

" I can, " said Genie, strongly.

Minaz and Kevin got out of sight. Genie sat near Jola who was laying on the ground, fainted. Minutes passed. Jola moved his head. Slowly, he opened his eyes. He sat up with great struggle. Genie did not make a single move. Jola looked at Genie, panting.

" Genie, " he said, " p - please - help - me... I'm - your - teacher... dear - Genie - let - me - escape - please – please... help - me... "

" Perhaps, I will let you escape, " said Genie.

" To the hell! " Genie added sharply, hitting Jola hard in the face with her elbow and he fell again, with a shriek. Genie became surprised at what she did.

Then, Kevin and Minaz came back. They were carrying green ropes in their hands.

" Where did you get those thick ropes? " Genie asked them.

" They're not ropes, " said Kevin. Genie raised her eyebrows.

" We just plucked some strong climber-plants, " explained Minaz.

They bounded Jola with the "wild green ropes" to the tree.

" Now, tell us, " said Minaz. Jola was completely unable to move, now.

" Please... I - know - nothing... " panted Jola.

" Don't tell jokes, tell us! " Minaz went forward and gave a punch on Jola's nose and the nose started to bleed.

" AAAAHH! " Jola shrieked.

" TELL US! " Minaz gave another punch o his nose.

" OUCH! " Jola screamed.

" TELL US! " Minaz began to give one more punch, but then Jola screamed :

" I will! I will! "

" Good, " Minaz took his hand away from him. Genie felt so bad.

" I - was - kidnapping - Anne. I - kidnapped - the - girl - to - get - Genie! " A jet of blankness shot through Genie's head.

" For what you were wanting Genie? " Kevin asked sharply.

" Wait, " said Minaz, " wait, Jola, where's the girl? "

" In - the - boat! " Jola said weakly.

" You came in a boat? " Genie asked.

" Yes! " Jola said.

" Where's the boat? Where? Where? " Minaz asked hurrily.

" Go - straight - and - you'll - see - a - river! There's - the - boat! " Jola answered.

Genie, Kevin and Minaz ran as fast as they could. They ran and ran and then they saw a river. They were on the bank of a wild river.

There was a boat on the edge of the water. The boat was tied to a tree on the bank with a rope. The three adventurers ran towards the boat.

There was a little girl with curly dark hair and dark eyes laying in the boat. She was bounded tightly to the floor of the boat with ropes. She was weak and pale. There were scratches over her hands and face. Her mouth was tightly covered with a plaster.

She struggled to say something when she saw Genie, Kevin and Minaz. But her mouth was covered. They jumped to the boat and unbounded her. They took the ropes and the plaster off.

" Ah, " panted the girl, tearfully.

" Anne? " Genie said kindly. The girl nodded weakly.

Genie, Kevin and Minaz helped Anne to sit up. She was too weak and tired and scared.

" Go and bring the Yumia girls, " said Minaz to Genie. Genie ran as fast as she could. At last, she got to the place where Maria and Merina were sitting. They got to their feet, when they saw Genie.

" Anne, " panted Genie.

" What? "

" Come with me! " Genie ran to the river with Maria and Merina behind her.

They got to the boat. Minaz and Kevin were comforting Anne.

" Anny! " Merina screamed. Anne looked up weakly and shrieked :

" Merrie! "

Merina sped forward and hugged Anne tightly. The two girls burst into tears.

" Anny... " sobbed Merina, touching Anne's wounded cheeks with shivering fingers.

" Merrie, I - I -" Anne could not say anymore. She sobbed into Merina's chest.

Genie felt her own eyes watering.

" We must punish Jola, " said Minaz.

" Yes, " said Merina with burning eyes.

" Come with me, " Minaz said to Genie.

Genie followed Minaz silently. As they walked through the woods, a mad thought came to Genie- was she starting to like Minaz? Oh, how can she be? Genie filled her mind with her dislike towards Minaz, because she was afraid if she would stop hating him.

They got near the tree where Jola was bounded.

" Where's he? " Genie squealed. There was no one bounded to the tree. The ropes that where bounding Jola were laying on the ground.

" Come! " Minaz said aloud and he ran into the bushes. Genie ran with him. They saw Jola disappearing into the woods.

" Catch him! " Minaz yelled. Genie and Minaz chased Jola.

Running and running and running and running... Genie was being wounded and scratched here and there by the sharp branches of the trees. She was being weak. But, still she ran. She was being covered in sweat. She felt her face burning and reddening.

Jola ran fast, but Genie and Minaz were faster than him. They got too close to Jola... they stretched their hands out to catch Jola... but, then, without a warning, Jola turned. He had a very sharp knife in his hands and Genie and Minaz stopped.

" Ha! What you thought? Did you believe I would be completely trapped if you bounded me with some stupid ropes? But... I have weapon, what you don't ! " Jola said and he laughed evilly.

" Now, I'm going to kill you two! " Jola held his knife to them.

Genie and Minaz made a swift move. They jumped forward and caught Jola. Jola was pinned to the ground. He tried to escape, but his knife had gone flying from his hand and landed on the ground, when they caught him.

" Get the knife! " Minaz yelled. Genie ran towards the knife.

Jola tried to get it. Minaz tried to stop him, but Jola kicked him aside and got to his feet. Genie looked back with great terror. Jola came running towards her. Genie ran as fast as she could... her hands will reach the knife in no time. But, Jola caught her and her hands narrowly missed the knife. Minaz was running towards them. But before he could reach them, Jola threw Genie cruelly. It was a strong move and Genie went flying. She hit a tree nearby. A great pain made her insides shudder. She felt bloody red. The wood was so hard... she was falling... she fell onto the ground...

Genie felt her eyes closing. She tried hard to hold them open. But the vision was blurring... her face was bleeding... every inch of her body was aching... The vision blurred and blurred... darkness... only darkness...

CHAPTER NINE
THE REAL ADVENTURE

Genie tried to open her eyes. But it was too difficult to open them. The pain was a little lightened, but it was still there. She felt herself moving... moving...

Genie opened her eyes. She found herself laying in a seat. A comfortable seat. She was back in the car..

" Oh, Genie, are you OK? " Kevin's panicked voice came from some far away planet. Genie tried to sit. A pair of hands came and helped her to sit up. She was sitting in the car of Minaz. There were Kevin, Maria, Merina, Antonella, Anne and Minaz in the car with her. Minaz was driving the car.

"What had happened to me? " Genie asked weakly. As she spoke, she felt her pain multiple.

" Aaah, " she shivered. Kevin sat near her, trying to comfort her. She rested her aching head on his shoulders. She felt warm teardrops running down her cheeks.

" Nothing... you just fainted and Minaz took you back to

us. " He said.

" Oh, Genie... are you alright? " Maria asked kindly.

" Give her some water, " said Merina. Genie closed her eyes. When she opened them again, a bottle filled with cool water was waiting for her in Kevin's hands. Genie took it with shuddering hands and drank. Her mouth was smarting, too.

Genie closed her eyes... maybe, sleep would rescue her from the pain...

When Geni woke, it was night. The sky was starry. She felt better. The pain was gone. She sat up with no help from others.

" How are you, now? " Anne asked her.

" I feel better, now, " said Genie.

" And - thank you, " said Anne, a little smile appearing in her lips.

" For what? " Genie asked truthfully.

" For saving me, " said Anne and she hugged Genie.

" Did Jola escape? " Genie asked, turning to Minaz.

" Yes, " said Minaz, " he escaped. "

Genie became disappointed.

" He disappeared into the forest. I searched for him. But he was gone, " sighed Minaz.

" And the reason of why he was wanting me?" Genie said eagerly.

" Who knows? " Minaz said and Genie felt strange.

" Jola did not tell us. He escaped, " said Minaz.

" Did he say how he kidnapped Anne? " Genie said.

" He didn't, but Anne did, " said Merina.

" Yes, Anne told us how that monkey kidnapped her, " said Kevin.

" I will tell you the story, " said Antonella enthusiastically,

" the night Anne came to Merina and Maria's house, Jola

broke into the compound of that house. He waited till everyone went to sleep. Then he threw a toy of a tiger into the room Anne was sleeping in. Anne heard a sound and woke and saw the toy coming flying in through the open window. She became curious."

"She took the toy and looked down through the window. Then she saw a rabbit. Jola was hiding behind a tree and he had brought the rabbit there. Anne became more curious. She was so sleepy, too. She got out of the house and went to the rabbit. Anne is so kind to animals, you know, she felt pity to the poor rabbit standing in the cold."

"Anne took the rabbit and turned to go back to the house. Right then, Jola came out and caught her. She tried to run and scream, but he hit her hard on the head with something ironic."

"Anne fainted. When she opened her eyes, she was in a van. By her description, we guessed it was Jola-Van. Jola was driving the van. Anne was bounded. Jola told her she have no chance to hope her parents will come to rescue her, because he had sent note to them saying she had just gone to find her tiger."

"Jola took her to a riverside. There was a man waiting for him. The man was guarding a boat. It seemed like Jola and the man were close friends. Jola and the man bounded Anne in the boat. And Jola got into the boat and they travelled for days."

"At last, they got into the South Forests. Jola left Anne in the boat, to check if we were there. And then you and Kevin and Mr Minaz found her. " Antonella finished historically.

Suddenly, the car shook dangerously and Anne slipped. But right then, Genie jumped and caught her and set her back in the seat, safely.

" Nice move, Genie. " Minaz said smilingly. Genie looked

at him, surprised.

" Thank you, Alfred, " She heard herself say in smiling-ly to Alfred Minaz. Kevin stared from Minaz to Genie, his mouth hanging open.

" So, the adventures end here, " said Merina.

" No, Merina, the adventures begin here. " Genie corrected her.

" What do you mean? " Merina asked her.

" We have to find out why Jola was against me. We have to find him for that, first. " Genie explained.

" I think we should take an interval befor we do that. Your parents would be waiting for you, all panicked, " said Minaz. They travelled for a long time. The night passed. No one slept.

And a new day dawned. They were away from the South Forests. They saw the top of the big house of the Yumias through the group of trees.

" You're right, Genie, " said Merina " the real adventures begin here! "